THE
FANTASY LEAGUE
MURDERS

DONALD DEWEY

MILFORD HOUSE

an imprint of Sunbury Press, Inc.
Mechanicsburg, PA USA

MILFORD HOUSE

an imprint of Sunbury Press, Inc.
Mechanicsburg, PA USA

For information about special discounts for bulk purchases, please contact Sunbury Press Orders Dept. at (855) 338-8359 or orders@sunburypress.com.

To request one of our authors for speaking engagements or book signings, please contact Sunbury Press Publicity Dept. at publicity@sunburypress.com.

ISBN: 978-1-62006-412-2 (Trade paperback)

Library of Congress Control Number: 2018937201

FIRST MILFRED HOUSE PRESS EDITION: March 2018

Product of the United States of America
0 1 1 2 3 5 8 13 21 34 55

Set in Bookman Old Style
Designed by Crystal Devine
Cover by Lawrence Knorr
Edited by Lawrence Knorr

Continue the Enlightenment!

For Pete McDonough

CHAPTER 1

With his usual eerie consistency, Mr. Black walked out of the Nerone woman's apartment building at 9:15, crossed the street to his blue Subaru and got in behind the wheel for his drive home. I counted to five before the light went out in the fourth-floor corner apartment of 24 Forest Avenue. Sometimes I had gotten as far as eight and nine, other times the window had gone dark before Black had reached his car. You must stay flexible in the investigation business, always be ready to roll with the vast varieties of human behavior.

And sometimes you also must shake up your own surveillance routine just to avoid going out of your mind. This time I decided to give Black a two-block lead before getting into gear. Since I had flanked him on the left parallel street of Ashby the last time, I decided to go for broke by swinging right from Edison to hit Adams four blocks away. Once I was back parallel to where Black should have been, I tore down Adams to the boulevard a mile away. Long John Silver couldn't have felt more adventurous as I imagined all the quickies Black was getting on his street without me there to observe and report back to Mrs. Black.

I arrived at the boulevard just as he was slowing down at Oak one block to my left. The light told me to keep moving, but I didn't want to have to cross the boulevard and continue all the way down to Merrick, then parallel him again for another couple of miles. So, I just waited for the light to change and for him to pass me. Even hilarity had its limits.

I stayed a block behind Mr. Black for the rest of the way to Lynbrook. It had become such a predictable run every Tuesday and Thursday night for the last month that I had fallen back on the same depressing philosophical question each time we had approached Hempstead Lake; to wit, after the doctor had delivered me and given me a slap on the ass, had he handed me over to my mother saying, "Here, Mrs. Finley, this is Paul who will one day follow Mr. Black around from his job to his lover and back to his wife?" I would have bet the answer was no, but the trouble with the Black case was that I had begun contemplating the question as a bettable proposition.

From the outset, Mrs. Black had made it clear I was to do nothing except pick up her husband when he left his office at 5:30 sharp on Tuesdays and Thursdays, follow him to his destination, sit there while he did what he did, then follow him home. She didn't want pictures, X-rays, anything. The only way I'd even found out Mr. Black's hostess was named Nerone had been to ignore Mrs. Black's instructions to stay in my car, not go near the lobby of 24 Forest Avenue. My reward for phoning in this information was a tirade by Mrs. Black that she would fire me if I ever again disobeyed her instructions. That had done it for my sense of initiative on the Black case.

Not that tailing errant husbands was the extent of my caseload. Sometimes there were errant wives, too, though not as often as my clients wanted. I've always been queasier about getting the goods on women because the husbands who have come to me with that problem are as likely as not to welch on my bill. There seems to be a male hormone that pumps out embarrassment and obstinacy in equal measure: embarrassment in coming to me in the first place, obstinacy once my reports have been handed over that I hadn't told them anything they hadn't already known. At least Mrs. Black made sure my check was in the mailbox every Saturday morning.

Back on Lakeview Avenue in Lynbrook, I slid into a sidewalk space until Mr. Black went into his garage, came out again, closed the garage, then bounced up to the front door. Normally, I signed off on a surveillance right then and there, if only not to forget the exact time. But Mrs. Black was as fastidious as her husband about schedules, and I knew I had 10 seconds tops for pulling out of my space and driving by her window so she could see I had been observing the terms of our agreement. Sure enough, she had her head under the shade, ready to pull it down, as I went by. Only then could I feel responsible in returning home to Garden City.

CHAPTER 2

As always, the Professor had every light on the two floors on in case an airliner lost its way to Kennedy. I had stopped griping to him about it, but it still scalded my Black Irish soul. The main reason I had stopped complaining was that it had done no good; another was that it was his house and he was paying the electric bills.

As soon as I saw Mary Reynolds sitting on the couch, I wanted to strangle the old man for more than keeping utility companies profitable. The soda cans and potato chips on the coffee table said he had once again been mixing his pleasure with my business.

"See, didn't I tell you, Mary? Only 10 minutes off tonight. What happened, Paul—Mr. Black have a flat tire?"

Mary Reynolds jumped off the couch like a cat who had been on a forbidden piece of furniture. "I'm sorry, Mr. Finley. I didn't realize it would be so late."

The Professor read my glare accurately and retreated to the personal bowl of potato chips he had on his stomach. "There's nothing new yet, Mary. I told you I'd call you if there was."

Mary Reynolds hadn't come so far or endured so many of the Professor's windy stories just to pick up her bag and leave. Instead, she handed me another photograph of her missing brother. "I found this today when I was doing some cleaning. I think it's more recent than the one I gave you."

Two lies: She hadn't just been doing some cleaning and she knew the picture was no more recent than the one I had given friends down at the precinct. I glanced at the same blond suburban kid who had once been 13 or 14 and who was now two years older, then shoved the picture in my pocket. "Want another soda, Mary? No? Then go home. You're not doing yourself any good like this."

Mary Reynolds was in her late twenties, but she had been worn down by more than those years. Even before Tommy Reynolds hadn't returned home from his part-time job at the video shop in the mall, she had skipped several years of her own youth by acting as both mother and father for her brother. As she crossed her thin arms to control a tremor, she seemed to have toted up all her dark thoughts about the illnesses that had taken away both her parents within two years of each other, about the times she had lectured Tommy about his skin magazines and cigarettes, and about the kid's disappearance, coming to the sum that absolutely everything had been her fault.

"Tommy's 16, Mr. Finley. But he's a very young 16. He just isn't somebody who'd go off without telling me."

"And we're going to find him for you. Aren't we, Paul?"

Mary Reynolds pretended not to see the daggers I was aiming at my father-in-law. I had little choice but to give her one of those buck-up smiles my high school baseball coach had practiced in telling me I was no longer the starting shortstop, then no longer the starting right fielder, then, finally, no longer on the team. What I was thinking was that Tommy Reynolds, Closet Rebel, had either hopped a freight train to California or was very dead somewhere and that I hadn't heard of freight trains to California in a very long time.

The Professor finally walked Mary Reynolds to the door. I flopped down on the couch and made sure not to look after them. I didn't want to see any more of her yearning glances over his shoulder. As soon as I heard the door close, I took the picture out of my pocket for another look. White T-shirt, jeans, and high-tops in a backyard. Posed against a wire fence. Smiling because he had been told to smile for Mary's camera. I hated pictures like that. They were always so ignorant of what was going to happen a few years later.

"You could've been a little more polite."

I pulled out my first cigarette in an hour. I always seemed to need a club of some kind when the Professor was about to launch into one of his Good Behavior sermons. "What the hell you think you're doing, Joe?"

"Me??!! Turn this place into an office, people see a light and assume it's business hours."

"That's not what I'm talking about, and you know it."

He thought that one over behind another sip of soda then lumbered over to the remote-control panel atop the TV set. "That girl's pulling off her skin because she's afraid something's happened and it's her fault. I think I'd give that a little more attention than who's fucking Mr. Black."

"Every cop on the Island is looking for Tommy Reynolds."

"Sure they are."

"Well, at least they know I'm looking for him."

"What about the city? We got 50 states. More than 200 countries not counting the Pacific territories and . . ."

"Joe!"

He finally seemed to remember he wasn't alone in the room with his ideas and indignations. He clicked on the TV to see Cary Grant running around with Katherine Hepburn and her leopard. "All I'm saying is that there's always somebody else to pester. Point me in the right direction, I'll do it myself."

"And suppose the kid's already dead?"

"Then find her the goddamn body!"

I had no answer to that. Even at the cost of giving Joe Carroll another last word, I still wanted to believe in freight trains to California. I grabbed a Coke from the refrigerator and went down to the basement. I liked it much more as my office at night than during the day. With the sunlight coming through the four ceiling-high windows, it looked like a well-furnished cellar bin that had just been cleared of coal. But at night the desk, file cabinets, and extra table took on the isolated comfort of a cavern. Caverns were my idea of happiness.

My most immediate task was to finish the transcription of my interview with Martin Morris, a heart specialist who had a penchant for terrorizing patients into operations he then botched. Malpractice suits, particularly those involving Gramercy Insurance, accounted for 75 percent of my business. It was tedious work, mainly turning on a tape recorder and asking formula questions, but it paid the supermarket bills more regularly than trailing after the Mr. Blacks of the world did. It also helped that Gramercy's chief claims man was Peter Piccolo, who co-founded our neighborhood baseball rotisserie league with me. He had apparently figured out from our first meeting that if he didn't keep sending work in my direction, he didn't stand a chance in hell of collecting from all the stupid trades I made with him during the fantasy season.

Piccolo wasn't going to be happy about Martin Morris, though. The doctor's latest victim, Bernard Albers, had proved more embarrassing than most because he had died on the operating table rather than at home a few weeks later and because the Widow Albers was the daughter of a German physician who had developed some precise ideas about when a malpractice suit was pursuable. I thought she had Morris and Gramercy Insurance by the balls. and intended slanting my report to Piccolo in that direction.

Apart from some occasional stakeout work by the Professor, Finley Investigations consisted entirely of Finley. This meant I not only conducted the interviews with the likes of Morris and members of the Albers family but also did all the transcriptions. In a bind, I farmed out some of the typing to a service in Hempstead, but I tried to work around binds. A, because I'm cheap. B, because the service is run by another ex-cop I had never liked when we had been on the job together. C, because I'm cheap.

And maybe there was a D, too. For the Professor, evenings meant *Bringing Up Baby, The Awful Truth,* or some other venerable black-and-white comedy on the tube. I didn't have the patience anymore for the golden oldies I'd seen a dozen times. When it wasn't baseball season, in fact, I watched television about as often as I fell in love . . . Okay, that's an exaggeration. The newest infant in a remote New Guinea village watches TV more than *that.* But camping down in front of the tube with the Professor at night would have represented too much suburban normalcy for me, and the last thing I wanted to accept was that living under Joe Carroll's roof was normal.

Three years before, we had drifted toward one another in pain and a thousand undeclared intentions of making it easier for one another. Maybe twice in all that time had we gotten down to a lengthy conversation about Jennifer (my wife, his daughter) and Susan (my daughter, his grandchild), and even on both those occasions I'd become so much more preoccupied with refusing to share his scotch that I had ended up feeling like a spectator to the choking tears the booze had drawn from him. If he had been just Joe Carroll, he would have taken those occasions as a final excuse for throwing his bottle at me or throwing me out of the house, at the very least noting that my inertia and self-loathing since the accident couldn't possibly have gotten any worse by being liquefied on the rocks. But because Joe Carroll had also spent too many years as a history guru for undergraduates at Adelphi, he was also the Professor who reached for his reason along with his Bromo the following morning and insisted on viewing my behavior within the context of the Age of Enlightenment.

So why hadn't *I* taken the initiative and gotten out? Why had *I* insisted on bubbling in memories that, at best, threatened to make me an emotional dwarf once and for all? When I was feeling relatively human, I told myself it was because I was still going to come through, that by some magic gift of tongues I would sit down one day with both Joe Carroll and the Professor and persuade both that none of us had been responsible for the deaths of Jennifer and Susan. When I was just being the Paul Finley I wanted to get along with, I told myself I would indeed move on—as soon as the old man wouldn't feel hurt by my leaving, as soon as I had enough money to open a proper office, as soon as I could wake up in the morning and believe it wasn't already too late to get going.

I turned on my tape recorder.

Let me ask you this, Dr. Morris. When the patient Albers asked whether you'd advise a second opinion about undergoing surgery . . .

I turned it off again. That was about as many words as I could handle at one go. As I pecked them out on my old keyboard letter by letter, I wondered if Martin Morris had also been operating on Tommy Reynolds.

CHAPTER 3

My first stop the next morning was to Kinko around the corner. Not once have I ever needed to refer to a malpractice interview, but I still felt better having a copy of the transcript in my files. It was the kind of superfluous thoroughness I had been known for as a cop, too.

Robinson was waiting outside the copy store for me, going through one of his routines about giving me a ticket for parking at the very edge of a bus stop. "Do it, Robby, and I'll send your wife a poison pen letter."

"See that red on the curb, Finley? A lot of paint went into that color."

I laughed, but more edgily than I would have a year before. At what point, I wondered, would the uniforms I had once worked with classify me as a civilian no longer entitled to their winks? "I'm going, I'm going. And I'll remember you on the holidays."

"Try my birthday. It's sooner."

I turned around to give him every tooth in my head before I pulled away. In another life, Robinson had been a weight-lifter whose sheer strength had shouldered the rotting beam of a dilapidated attic on Crestview and Lark while I had yanked out a doper who had brought the building down around his ears by overdoing the paraffin. In this life, he looked like just another overweight patrolman trudging out the groundball toward his pension. I promised myself I *would* remember him at Christmas.

I drove to Gramercy to deliver the transcript of my *tête-à-tête*
with Morris. The company was quartered in a three-story red
brick building that seemed to be a compromise between the architect's inner city public school background and his new-found
philosophy that Sterile Is Good. The lobby had everything but
light and the elevator to the third floor nothing but Ray Coniff
brought back still again by some new digital miracle. Gramercy's
reception area was more of the same lobby dimness, but with a
young receptionist instead of an Uncle Willie security guard. She
was busy collating papers with lots of statistics and shot her jaw
up at me as though I might have been a number to be included
belatedly. She was also about the sixth or seventh receptionist I
found it necessary to introduce myself to. When I had mentioned
this turnover to Piccolo around the time of Number Five, he had
done nothing but grunt.

In fact, Pete Piccolo was an unending series of grunts. I had
met him originally while processing the claim for Jennifer's accident. Maybe he had only been doing his job in sending me the
check Jennifer had been contributing toward every first of the
month for 12 years, but he had done it tactfully, with none of
that touchy-feely bleat some commercial agents presume is their
right to enclose with the cash. Then one night, a couple of months
after the funeral, I had run into him at the Dover Bar and Grill,
and we had managed to strike up a conversation having little to
do with Jennifer and Susan and a lot to do with a messy divorce
he was going through. It was probably the only time in my life I
hadn't minded listening to somebody else's problems in a saloon.
If nothing else, I had thought that evening, he had assumed I was
ready to acknowledge other people also had problems.

One thing had led to another. I had quit the department with
no clear idea of what I intended doing next, Gramercy had been
looking for an investigator. Just as important, he had claimed to
know all there was to know about Ty Cobb, Jackie Robinson, and
Pete Rose. This had led to our first rotisserie league, with some
wise guys from his office, two neighbors of mine, and the Professor. Thanks to Piccolo's presence, I also hadn't been the most
steamed member of the pool when the Professor had walked off
that first year with more than $1,200 in winnings.

That had been then. Sitting behind his desk with the transcription of the Morris interview, Piccolo looked too grave ever to be seen in a bar like the Dover. The fact was, he had gone straight from his divorce and a vicious custody battle over his two children to the No Fun House. There was a heaviness to his movements now that all his manic health regimes seemed only to accentuate. I couldn't imagine this Peter Piccolo ever being a help during a policy settlement.

"This typist is as messy as the last one."

"Nobody good wants to do hack work anymore."

He considered a smile, then thought better of it. "Final score?"

"Dr. Morris is a very busy man. All those golf games to play, so many beating hearts to transplant. When Albers asked about a second opinion, Morris coughed up the legal answer to cover his ass."

"But?"

"But Dr. Morris has a deskside manner like Torquemada."

"Who?"

Another minute too long listening to the Professor's monologues. "An old Italian. Anyway, Morris even made me jumpy, and I didn't have Albers' cardiogram."

"But he didn't explicitly discourage a second opinion."

"C'mon, Pete. The guy didn't have to be explicit. Albers had enough problems without irritating the white coat that was about to cut into his pump."

"So you're saying?"

"Give the widow something and jack up the rates on Morris."

"Just like that."

"Be good p.r."

"That's another department." He glanced at the transcript for what looked like the last time, then set it aside on his desk. "Have time for something else?"

"I mean it, Pete. There's no way Morris didn't intimidate the old man."

"I'll mention it to Legal. You want something else or not?"

One of the less attractive features of three-piece suit vests is that they have breast pockets that accommodate the thumbs while viewing the world as a circus of acrobatic dogs. Piccolo had been wearing his vests a lot lately—which meant I'd been taking out more cigarettes than normal in his presence to regain my leverage with him. "What's this butcher's name?"

He reached reluctantly into a drawer and came out with a glass ashtray. "No malpractice. A movie theater." He spun around in his leather chair for a dossier on the shelf behind him and tossed it in front of me. "A lady says she slipped and fell. Says it was because the floor was sticky."

I didn't need to read the name of the theater twice. It was a porno house that had gone through several reincarnations as Long Island's biggest art theater, Long Island's home of karate and kung-fu, and Long Island's bastion of all the golden oldies the Professor watched for free at home.

"A *woman* fell?" I couldn't help asking.

For once, Piccolo thought something was genuinely funny.

CHAPTER 4

Because of the unannounced visit by Mary Reynolds, I had something to do after leaving Piccolo besides going home and getting back to a transcript for a dentist named Hammond. Not that I expected a 21-gun salute when I walked into the station house. Miles and Levine were already smarting about my involvement in Tommy Reynolds's disappearance, and I understood their attitude only too well. When I had been in their place, I had regarded a private investigator as a pain in the ass paid in direct proportion to the number of irritating visits and phone calls he made. By that standard on the Reynolds case, Miles and Levine saw me as a millionaire.

Every time I walked into the bullpen and saw Ellen sitting at my old desk, I wanted to tell her to get up and go back to her own workstation. The least she could have done, I thought, was to have rearranged her In and Out boxes or gotten a new phone. Change should have been change.

"We gave last week," she said, as soon as she saw me.

Sitting at the flanking desk, Levine had seen me a second before Ellen. This was time enough for him to go through a series of peevish expressions culminating in a toss of his pencil in the air. "Or maybe you came here to give *us* something this time?"

"Thanks, I'm fine. How about you guys?"

"I told you we'd call . . ."

I had the new old picture out before I heard myself apologizing for what I didn't want to apologize for. "The sister says this one's more recent. I'm not sure about that, but it can't hurt, right?"

Ellen did me the favor of accepting the photograph, trying to work up interest in it, then wheeling her chair over to drop it on Levine's desk. That was more than Levine would have done if I had made the mistake of giving him the picture first.

"Looks like the same Tommy Reynolds to me," he said.

"The sister's grasping, you know?"

"So you got her going through the house for First Communion pictures so she'll feel like she's doing something?"

"You're not funny, Herb."

Ellen sensed a moment for diplomacy. "Take it over, Herb. Like he says, it can't hurt."

Levine stood up as if being raised by pulleys. The years had only hardened his dislike of the one-time superior who had written in one annual evaluation that he might have been a good foot soldier, but that he had as many leadership qualities as Howdy Doody. At the time, it had seemed like a funny observation. "Sure," he said. "We run a 24-hour printing service. Get your pictures and bring 'em on down."

We both waited for Levine to drag himself over to Photography. "You were a lot more fun when you worked around here, Paul. Now it's touchy, touchy."

And non-touchy, touchy, I thought. After so much time I still didn't know if there might have been more than one night with Ellen Jovanko if the accident hadn't happened. I was never going to find out, either—not after her marriage to one of Nassau County's rising assistant prosecutors who spent his downtime marching alongside bishops and holy rollers to protest abortion clinics. Now that Ellen Jovanko had been reborn as Ellen Miles and several other things, she had absolutely no reason to remember what had happened or might have happened, in her past life.

"Tommy Reynolds your only work these days?"

"You must have come up with *some*thing."

She registered the evasion, then shrugged. "Nobody at the video store knows anything. Nobody in the mall knows anything. His school friends say he was acting normally. The sister checks out. The uncle and aunt in Philadelphia say they talked to both just a few days before the disappearance, detected nothing. The neighbors . . ."

"Okay, okay. But he's still 16. The bloom of high school . . ."

"That wasn't a bloom."

"So he just ran off? Got high somewhere and tried to fly off a tall building and you just haven't found the body?"

She gave both of us a chance to count to five, then slipped a folder out from under the pile on her desk. "See?" she said, opening it to show me the first picture I had given her. "Right here in front of me. You'll hear a minute after I hear."

I muttered something like an apology, then spotted a skel sitting at a corner desk, trying to look efficient about his paperwork. "Who the hell's that?"

Ellen didn't bother turning around. "McGowan."

"Vacation fill-in?"

"Not exactly," she said, addressing her desk blotter. "They keep telling him there's a bottle waiting for him at his next transfer. As long as he doesn't catch up to it, he keeps his shield."

My self-pity sprang to life. McGowan had it easy, it said: He could blame booze for his entire life, I could blame it for only one night.

CHAPTER 5

I got to the Cameo the following evening around seven. Once upon a time, its oversized marquee had probably looked out of place as a Manhattan import hanging over a narrow Long Island sidewalk; in the DVD age, it looked as much out of time as out of place. The township seemed to have agreed. Although the theater was only a few storefronts off the main street, it might as well have been in the woods that started further down the hill. The only other signs of commerce on the street were a card collector's shop across the way and a lumber company next door. The rest of the decline was taken up by an abandoned firehouse, a warehouse of some kind, and facing lots with For Sale signs posted on the rusted chicken wire. With the two stores closed, the marquee had been left with the task of providing the only light for the block.

I sat behind the wheel for a few minutes trying to whip up enthusiasm for my latest Gramercy client. After spending most of the day with Dr. John Hammond's slipshod oral surgery practices, I figured I had some variety—maybe even creative investigation—coming. And there was one that struck me right away. The Cameo's program for the evening consisted of WHEN BAD GIRLS ARE REALLY BAD, THE HOBO AND THE TRAMP, and something identified only as SPECIAL FEATURES. But there was also a little announcement on the bottom line of the marquee saying that the theater offered THE BEST IN KUNG-FU EVERY FRI AND SAT NITE. Checking the file on one Joanna Mendler that Piccolo had given me, I saw that Gramercy's latest litigant claimed to have hurt herself on a kung-fu, not a porn, night. I didn't know exactly what that told me about Joanna Mendler, but I liked the idea that I had worked out that detail for myself rather than through another tedious interview.

Since it had the gall to stay in business against accepted business wisdom, the Cameo had thought nothing about going all the way by charging fifteen bucks for a ticket. As I tucked the stub into my shirt pocket, I was beginning to smell a lot more to the place than porn *or* kung-fu. Or was that just the usual effect entering a movie house had on me—the action on the screen just one, not the only, fantasy set into motion?

I got through the lobby without spotting any roaches, then ran into Boardman, who was bent over a Coke machine and scooping out a few dollars' worth of quarters. At least I assumed it was Boardman: The file hadn't said anything about an assistant manager.

"Remember—no smoking."

Even as a cop, I had never issued an order like that without looking at the person. But Boardman, a squat 40-year-old with a blond crewcut, kept counting his coins. "What's that laying over there?"

He had the grace to interrupt his counting, size me up as somebody who wasn't after his loot and glance over to the Parliament butt I was pointing to. He still wasn't impressed. "That was a mistake," he said. "We learn from our mistakes. Don't be a mistake."

When he immediately went back to his quarters, I decided he deserved the first round.

The orchestra was bursting with as much business as the street had promised: only about four or five single males and a couple giggling away at some guy who was hung like Neptune plowing away at a .35mm ass. The place smelled like it had been drowned in strawberry deodorant. The sight of the broken EXIT signs on either side of the screen raised my arm hairs again about something going on apart from movies. Any developer with enough clout and $100 to invest in the street could have used even the dead bulbs in the EXIT signs to start condemnation proceedings.

Or had the fire department next door done just that and found *itself* out of business? I was beginning to like the Cameo theater a lot.

I took an aisle seat near the back, at the top of the rise in the floor where Joanna Mendler had supposedly fallen and hurt her leg. An old-timer two rows in front looked back to see if I was his wife, decided I wasn't and went back to the frolics up on the screen. I took out my pocket flashlight and, palming it so it didn't give off a glare, played it on the floor. Mendler had been right about one thing: There was enough guck on the floor to make a Braille map of the world. On the other hand, I didn't see any especially sneaky ridges. So, what kind of shoes had she been wearing? What about the soles?

I turned off the flashlight and sat back to devise more Maigret-like questions. They came a lot more slowly than Neptune and his blonde friend with the enormous thighs. Everything still seemed to come down to one thing: What the hell was a 35-year-old woman with an address in the glitzy Golden Cove section of the Island doing in the Cameo on a Saturday night, to begin with? If I suspected Piccolo of a sense of humor, I might have thought he was giving me a special exam to see if I was still up to Gramercy's standards.

I caught Boardman in his office at the right moment, just after the first drag on his joint when his self-righteousness lacked conviction. "Hey, what is this barging in here!"

"You're Boardman, right?"

"And who the hell are you?"

I regretted having to close the door behind me. Even the strawberry deodorant outside was better than the rain-soaked paper that passed for air in Boardman's closet. "Gramercy Insurance."

"At this hour?"

"Twenty-four/seven your problems are our problems."

Boardman seemed to remember he owed me one from the lobby. He also concluded I was no reason to clip off his joint. "That dizzy broad last weekend? Look, I get threatened with a suit, so I tell you. Everybody going through the motions because that's how traffic flows. But I'll bet we don't hear another word about it."

"The lady's hired a lawyer, hasn't she?"

"Yeah. And I've got Perry Mason. We're going to fight this one all the way to the Supreme Court. Mr. . . .?"

"Finley. Gramercy wants to know why it should help you foot Mr. Mason's bill."

The sight of my tape recorder usually brought one of two responses: alarm that any further bullshit could (and would) be used against the party being interviewed or alarm that it had already recorded bullshit while sitting in my pocket. Boardman's reaction as I put the machine on his desk was to take another drag. "Believe me, Finley, there'll be no bill. When this broad wises up, Gramercy will be out your *per diem*, nothing else."

"Mrs. Mendler says she tripped and suffered an injury to a knee on your property. I was just inside. It's a wonder she didn't get the plague."

"Hey, whose side you on?"

I wouldn't have said no to a toke, but it wasn't being offered, so I settled for a Merit. Boardman took that to mean I wasn't just going to go away. "You're ruining a peaceful interlude here, Finley," he said, squashing the entire joint in his plastic triangle of an ashtray. "Okay. Mrs. Mendler. The kind they call Sheena, Bitch of the Jungle. The party around the indoor pool got boring. The hors-d'oeuvres were off. So, she staggered off into the night for another kind of thrill. Ended up here."

"You're stating for the record Mrs. Joanna Mendler appeared to be under the influence of some chemical substance?"

"Want me to say that? I'll say that."

"I'm *asking*, Boardman! Tell me what happened."

"There's nothing to tell, for Christ sake! I'm out in the lobby . . ."

"On Saturday the 14th."

"Whatever. I'm out there thinking a hundred profound things, she comes out holding herself. Says she fell, where can she sit. I bring her in here."

"Did you offer to call a doctor?"

"For what? My kid gets bigger scrapes falling in his sandbox."

"Did she ask you to call a doctor?"

"Just a cab."

"She didn't have her own car?"

Boardman shrugged. "It was a nice night. She probably staggered here on her own feet from the pool party."

I hated to break eye contact with him, but I had to confirm something with Piccolo's file. "She lives 10 miles away."

"What can I tell you?"

She might not have walked away from a pool party, I thought, but she certainly sounded like she had walked away from a friend with a car. "While she was here, she never made any threats to sue or anything?"

"Not a word. I put her in the cab, and the next thing I hear is this registered letter from her lawyer on Monday."

"You didn't make any moves on her, did you?"

Boardman slumped down even further in his chair; he seemed to be getting more comfortable in his clutter with every question. "I'll admit the thought was there."

"So?"

"So this," he said, waving a flabby hand at the peeling posters and old reel cans on the floor. "This is a small space, Finley. But as small as it is for you and me right now, it was even smaller when she was sitting where you are because she wasn't alone. She came in with somebody else in her head, and whoever it was made it really cramped in here. I couldn't wait to get rid of her."

"Conclusion?"

"She was out to make trouble for somebody. I was more convenient than the other guy. At least with me, she's got that scrape on her knee to see. Know what I mean?"

CHAPTER 6

I was glad to get out of Boardman's office and out of the Cameo altogether. When a guy like that began sounding perceptive about something, it was time to change location, and fast. Since I still had my juices going about the very survival of the theater, I took a few minutes to wander around for closer looks at the two lots, the firehouse, the warehouse, and the card and lumber stores. Ten minutes later, I had concluded that the Cameo shared its grim block with two lots, a firehouse, a warehouse, and the card and lumber stores. If Joanna Mendler's fall was the first step in some real estate grab scheme, the asphalt was as much in the dark about it as I was. On the principle of never quitting when behind, I then followed my feet up to the avenue. It was Anytown, Long Island, with all the Pizza Hut, McDonald's, and Hallmark signs where they should have been. The only note of semi-originality was a restaurant called the Coq d'Or. From the window, it looked much tonier than places where the French began and ended with the name—white tablecloths, candles, even a maître d' returning my peering from the end of a nose as long as the Eiffel Tower. I couldn't see us ever holding one of our fantasy baseball league sessions at the Coq d'Or.

Since it was a Thursday, I had to get out to the Nerone apartment to make sure Mr. Black got home safely. I was running later than I had promised the Professor, but I figured he had enjoyed every minute of picking up Black from his office, following him to Forest Avenue, and then settling down with a book on the

Medicis. The only thing I turned out to be wrong about was the book; it was a history of the Huns. "Just like you said," he said when I walked up to his old Chevy. "Straight here from the office. Where you been?"

"Porno movie."

"Educational, I hope."

I looked up at the familiar light in the corner apartment on the fourth floor of #24. "Some people do it, some watch others do it."

"So what's that make us down here? And what's it make your client?"

I had been asking myself those questions in one form or another since taking the job. But coming from the Professor, they suddenly sounded different. "She just wants to know from an intermediary what somebody else *might* be doing," I heard myself saying.

"The power of self-denial."

But of course, that was exactly what it wasn't. Self-denial would have never involved me or at most netted me a day or two of following Mr. Black. "I've been missing something here, Joe."

I was already halfway across the street to #24 before his puffing caught up with me. "I thought she asked you to stay away from them."

My sudden bravado told me the running gag was this: that somewhere along the line I had begun letting my cases tell me what was going on, with no interference from me. Once I had received my instructions from Mrs. Black, Pete Piccolo, even Mary Reynolds, I had assumed everything they had said was true and complete and it was only for me to act like a hired witness with a tape recorder. Even Boardman had been more skeptical of the facts thrown in his lap than I had been. If I had acted the same way as a cop, I would have still been handing out traffic tickets.

I got the vestibule door open with my last good Visa card. Warming to some unexpected action, the Professor got to the bells before I did. "Nerone?"

"Right."

He found it, then slapped my hand away from the bell with some new inspiration. "Holy shit! Nerone, Black! Black, Nerone!

Why didn't I see it before? It means the same thing, Paul! Lots of Italians used to anglicize their names!"

I didn't know the significance of that unless it meant Mr. Black was screwing some cousin, but the information dismayed the Professor enough to let me get to the bell on the second try. "Especially the Italian Jews," he said, slipping into lectern mode. "Many of them had never seen a church in their lives, but once they got over here, they figured they had problems enough being Italians without throwing in they were also Jews . . ."

The buzzer sounded, and I opened the door to the lobby with an order for him to wait for me. He was peeved not to go up with me, but he was already panting heavily and I knew that whatever else was waiting for me on the fourth floor, some kind of lie was. I've yet to meet the liar who has reacted happily to being found out.

Small as the elevator was, it made a lot of noise in sliding open on the fourth floor. Mr. Black was poised in front of the apartment at the end of the hall. Instead of the drab suits I had seen him in, he looked like Robert DeNiro from *The Godfather* in his spaghetti-strapped undershirt. "Yes?"

"Mr. Nerone?"

His answer came a second too late: I saw the old woman propped up on an armchair in the living room behind him as he said: "No, there's only my mother, Mrs. Nerone. Who are you?"

I thought about saying the Donkey's Ass. "Marriage counselor," I blurted.

"What?"

I told myself to cool it, that the worst should be saved for later while I was reflecting on the pivotal role of Finley Investigations in world affairs. "Your wife wanted me to drop by and make sure her mother-in-law was okay. Please tell her I think everything's fine and she'll get my final bill in a day or two."

Since I had nothing more even nearly that coherent to say, I turned and headed right back toward the elevator. This was good for a burst of Italian from the old woman, which got Black's motor running down the corridor. The elevator door turned out to be not only noisy, but slow, and a big loafer in the way made it useless altogether.

"I asked you something," Black said, no longer curious or polite.

"Ask your wife, Mr. Black."

"What do you know about my wife?"

"*Chiama la polizia, Johnny! Chiama la polizia!*"

That much I understood even from rolling my eyes over the original Italian in the Professor's copies of Dante. Then Black ruined my witty departure by reaching into the elevator car and grabbing me by the jacket. I was glad he did.

"She's had you following me!"

"Take it up with her."

"I'll take it up with you!"

There was too much of Mr. Black for the elevator door when he yanked back his left arm. Before he could get it back past the interference detector, I shot my own left hand out toward anything at all between his gut and double chin. I caught him below the Adam's apple—not necessary and not especially satisfying, but it was enough to retrieve my jacket front and send him moaning back against the hall wall. For a second, I was afraid I had really hurt him. He grabbed for his throat as though choking and went all wobbly against the wall. But then, with the old lady still screaming out at him from her chair, he started muttering again.

I smashed the L button as hard as I could, daring the door to slow down on me again. "Lot of people seem to want to hang on to you, Black. I'm not one of them."

The elevator door finally got the message: It rolled closed before I had to hear any more Italian from the mother or any more gasping from Mr. Black.

CHAPTER 7

I gave the Professor a choice of a Mama's Boy who had to see his mother in secret because of a hostile wife, a wife who was toting up her husband's minutes with a mother-in-law for some future alienation suit, or a wife who just wanted to be EXTREMELY sure her husband was where he claimed every Tuesday and Thursday. The good part of the drive home was that we had separate cars, so I didn't have to hear Joe debating the choice he preferred. The better part was getting home and tearing down to the basement to do the best typing of my life on Mrs. Black's bill. The best part of all was feeling so satisfied by my typing job that I didn't have room to think about a 44-year-old under the delusion he had been chasing after flies for a living when in fact he had been pursuing gnats.

Then the Professor spoiled the moment by clomping downstairs with a beer in his hand and settling down on the next to the bottom step. "You should hit this Black woman for everything she's got," he said.

"I don't want everything she's got."

He sipped his beer; he was saluting himself for holding back a whole 10 seconds. Then, finally: "Where the hell do you find them?"

"We're eating."

"That's what I like about you—your lofty view of things."

"Go to bed, Joe. You've got *Key Largo* to watch tomorrow."

Beer off a duck's back. "This other major case—the porn movies. What's that about?"

"I'm not in the mood right now."

"C'mon."

I gave him the Cameo story in five words; it seemed like too many.

"Was it a porn night or a martial arts night she had her fall?"

"Kung-fu. She likes to make war, not love."

"You mean she likes to see war. What else?"

"She seems to have nothing better to do on a Saturday night."

"More."

"I know, I know. None of it makes much sense."

"Then say it, for Christ sake. Get it out front."

He was right; even Boardman seemed like a happier thought than Mr. and Mrs. Black. "The creep at the movie house makes her sound like one part Medea and one part Holly Golightly."

"She has her children for breakfast at Tiffany's?"

"And she doesn't give a damn who knows she goes to the Cameo on Saturday nights. I mean, even if she was incensed that night, she carries it over to Monday. Image is not a priority here."

"Usually isn't with the very, very rich. So they tell me."

My eyes chose that moment to fall on the photo of Jennifer and Susan in the back corner of the desk. I had taken it at Niagara Falls five years before. Jennifer was standing against the railing exactly where the Falls broke and plunged, her long fingers on Susan's shoulders and the tiniest wince in her smile, as though wary the water might change direction behind her back. Susan looked completely contrary; she knew her mother's hands were as much for reining her in as for posing for a shot of two pals. I remembered snapping that picture, and I remembered there had been a soda vendor to my right. I could still see the neck of a Sprite bottle coming out of the vendor's ice.

"I don't think about them as much as I used to, Joe."

"Why should you? It's three years."

I felt brave about staring him down. "I'm *tired* of thinking about them."

He nodded unhesitatingly. "Sometimes I like thinking that where they are, they're tired of thinking about us, too."

I hadn't dared think that; I was still measuring my courage in drips. "There goes our cheering section."

It seemed to take him forever to lift his bulk off the step. I counted every fraction of it so I wouldn't miss the building of his anger. When he finally short-armed his beer can over the banister at me, I was ready for it, catching it perfectly before it could tip over my desk. A single splash up from the hole didn't seem nearly enough.

"Jennifer was my only daughter, Mr. Finley. Susan was my only grandchild. I have nothing coming after them. You still might have. So, save me your bullshit."

He went upstairs and disappeared through the door to the kitchen. He had never looked so hunched over or sounded so disdainful toward me. I thought it right to share that victory with Mr. and Mrs. Black, so I saluted them with a taste of beer. After all, we had just wound up a case together, hadn't we?

CHAPTER 8

For all my years on the Island, I remembered only four previous trips to the Golden Cove. Three had been on the same case: the kidnapping of the five-year-old son of a toothpaste baron. Although the FBI had commandeered the investigation from the start, Miles and I had gotten into it because we had developed independent evidence about the gambling debts of a family chauffeur—a particular that ultimately led to a confession and the safe return of the boy. The only other time I had used one of the Cove's golden knockers had been to see Judy Oettel—an obsession from the afternoon she had watched me trying out for the Adelphi lacrosse team, had winced to see me take a hard fall, and had then walked her tan legs and white socks away because she had absorbed all the tragedy she was capable of absorbing that day. I might not have made the team, but I had been resolved to get the consolation prize of a date with Judy Oettel. It had fallen to a houseman to inform me she had been down only for a few days and had returned to Brown in Rhode Island.

In other words, I told myself I was right at home as I followed the winding, cobblestone path around to the entrance of Joanna Mendler's estate. I might not have known much about the flowers and trees that seemed already in full sprout in late March, but I knew that if God had given Joanna Mendler and her legion of gardeners a dispensation from the seasons, I could also count on special understanding for my wants and needs.

Not.

A maid named Hanna looked me up and down at the door as though she hadn't expected me to be *that* grubby looking, then walked me around to the back from the outside so my shoes wouldn't come into contact with any rugs or carpets. Boardman had been wrong about the indoor pool, but there was an outside one—now being cleaned out by two guys in labeled blue jump-suits. Also waiting for me was Robert Chichester, a big roast beef of an attorney in a pinstriped suit and silk yellow tie who shook my hand as a gesture to Brotherhood Week. Then, of course, I had to be introduced to the lady of the house.

First impression? She scared the wits out of me. Long, cool, gaunt where it always showed, not so gaunt where propriety said it shouldn't. That afternoon, most of it showed because she was seated regally in an upright veranda chair, a denim shirt opened over a black bikini. The only other thing on her was a medicinal bandage on her left knee. I got plenty of looks at that since she had both legs raised on another chair to make sure none of us lost track of the central theme. By my twentieth glance, I could make out the faintest trace of raspberry polish sticking to the nail of her big toe.

Neither Chichester nor his client displayed the least surprise when I laid my recorder on the table. I reciprocated by showing none of my own when Chichester produced his own recorder from an attaché case and set it next to mine. We smiled at each other over our ice teas.

Chichester agreed that asking the lady her name and address was reasonable. He looked more irked at her for owning up read-ily to her 35 years—not because she admitted them, but because she could be so cavalier about the good 15 years separating them. I decided some unrequited love or greed was going on in front of me.

She repeated the facts more or less as Boardman had re-counted them. The big difference was that whereas my questions had worn out the theater manager's taste for his joint, Joanna Mendler polished off a tall gin and tonic and immediately sum-moned Hanna to get her a refill. I took that as a good sign for Piccolo and Gramercy.

"It's the disrespect, Mr. Finley," she said to me as the maid went off on her assignment.

"Disrespect?"

"For the patrons. It's a public entertainment facility. They charge good money for renting their broken seats for a couple of hours. All right, they're not in the upholstery business. But not even being able to walk up an aisle without tripping over a hill of come?"

Algae or no algae, Chichester looked like he wanted to jump into the pool.

"Cum, sperm," she repeated. "Whatever these men drop on the floor between Sunday and Thursday."

"You mean the porn nights."

"You know very well what I mean."

Chichester remembered why he was there. "Of course it doesn't matter what the actual sticky material was. The theater sells soda and . . ."

"I know what it was, Robert."

"I'm sure you do, Joanna. I'm just trying to make the point to Mr. Finley that the nature . . ."

It felt like my turn. "I'd bet it was soda."

She seemed to have been waiting for nothing else. It was her cue to reach over to the table for a Marlboro. There was no grimace from the pressure on her knee. "Why do you say that, Mr. Finley?"

By the time I got my matches out, she had already flicked her lighter. "Nobody leans out into an aisle to jack off."

"I take your point. Unless . . ."

"It all just oozed out there from inside the row? No, I don't think so. Wrong chemistry."

"You sound like an expert."

"We all pick up things here and there."

"Then we can agree we're talking about soda?"

Chichester's mediation came just in time. I had run out of wit, and she suddenly looked like she regretted something. I couldn't help thinking that maybe she was sorry she had twitted the sad little visitor with his tape recorder. Just that possibility made me mad. "Assuming we're talking about anything at all, Mr. Chichester. We still haven't received Mrs. Mendler's X-rays."

"You will."

"How about today?"

"I can't authorize . . ."

"Give him the X-rays, Robert." She was back to her stiff politeness with me. "I certainly don't want new ones made. My knee might look better."

"Heal fast, do you?"

Now she was simply unamused; I had crossed some boundary. And Chichester was quick to seize on my gaffe. "Anything else we can help you with, Mr. Finley?"

"Mrs. Mendler's shoes might be nice."

"Excuse me?"

"Heels can break off at the worst times."

"I was wearing pumps with a minimal heel."

"Right. Because you walked 10 miles from here to the Cameo."

"Because short men seem embarrassed when I walk past them."

Why did I have to remind myself under her stare that I was 6'1"? "Low heels are also good if you're prone to dizzy spells."

"Mrs. Mendler's health is perfect," Chichester cut in.

"Which your doctor will attest to?"

She nodded. "Of course."

"No reason for pills, anything like that?"

She figured her silence was enough of an answer. And why press that point when I still had so many others? "And you just take a gin and tonic when you're home here like today?"

"Your visit is a special occasion, Mr. Finley. I'll probably have a second before dinner tonight."

"You mean a third."

"A third," she said, almost graciously. "Before dinner."

"Rich food?"

"Not when I make it. If somebody invites me out, at times."

The lack of a car still didn't make sense. "Who invited you out on the 14th?"

I was so intent on making sure she knew my attention would be waiting for her that I didn't follow her glance at Chichester.

It occurred to me only later that his failure to intervene again at that point was curious. "Mel Gibson, actually," she finally said. "We had dinner together, I gorged myself on liquor, spices, and vertigo pills, then I said goodnight to him because I wanted to see *Masters of Peril*."

The title of the picture had been left out of Piccolo's file. That was the precious new fact I grasped as Hanna served the gin and tonic and left again. "So how was *Masters of Peril*?"

"Not as much style as I'd hoped."

Chichester leaned over the table to remind me what he looked like; his breath smelled of Dentyne. "Why Mrs. Mendler went to the theater is immaterial," he declared emphatically.

"You mean there's no VCR in the house here?"

"Of course there is," she said, cutting off another Chichester sulk. "My late husband believed that if somebody invented something and somebody else went to the trouble of marketing it, it was his duty to buy it."

I tried not to think of the palsied old man Mr. Mendler must have been. "Then why not rent *Masters of Peril* and watch it here?"

Another ambush. "I like the coming attractions at a theater," she said promptly. "They're always better than the movie you're there to see. Why do you think that is, Mr. Finley?"

Actually, it was an existential question I had meditated upon more than once. And I knew the answer. "Expectations."

For the umpteenth time, she threw me: She looked absolutely impressed. "Yes," she said, keeping me in view all the way to the ashtray. "Something like that."

She tapped off a long ash that hit more of the edge than the middle of the ceramic ashtray. She not only had a speck of raspberry polish on her toenail, I noticed, she also had the tiniest gray floater in her left eye.

I thought about the expectations of the dog that chased after the bus.

CHAPTER 9

Twenty-four hours later, I still didn't have the faintest idea of what I had learned from my interview with Joanna Mendler. None of my usual debriefing tactics worked—not the one where I sat in the basement to play and replay the interview; not the one where I played the person interviewed and the Professor cross-examined me; especially not the one where I tried to think of anything else but the subject at hand so I could bolt awake in the middle of the night and shout "I've got it! I've got it!" to the ceiling. I still had nothing but a very rich, seemingly very self-assured widow of 35 who had gone into a movie house she should have never gone into and who was suing a movie house she should have wanted to forget about. If the Widow Mendler had been one of my malpractice cases, I thought, she would have given me a tour of her liquor cabinet and showed me how much she consumed between operations. *She wanted something to happen to her!*

But not even that train of thought gave me more than a few seconds of epiphany since its natural follow-up was that she wanted *me* to happen to her. That consoled me that I still had my libido after years of moping around in my mental monastery, but it didn't shed much light where it would have done some practical good. The answer, I decided, was to shake down Piccolo for a few more bucks to dig further into Joanna Mendler.

Every weekday, noon sharp, Piccolo went directly from his office to the athletic club in Rockville Centre. The club was one of those places that divided the world into members and non-members. The first time I had gone there to see Piccolo, I hadn't told him ahead of time, so the preppie in a yacht captain's jacket at the door had gone through enough phone calls around the building to track down a cosmonaut drifting around in space. And every time his finger had come down on a button, he had sneaked me a glance that said he hadn't taken the job to help non-members like me. This time, though, I had called Piccolo first, so my name had been blocked out on a sheet that said GUESTS. Captain Andy had little choice but to use his finger to point out an elevator that would take me up to what he called the "competition room."

The "competition room" was an entire floor of squash and handball courts, a gym, and various other arenas for shedding managerial flab. Even the usual odors of liniment and rancid workout clothes seemed buttoned up within separate compartments, the L-shaped corridor around them a walk through invisible cherry blossoms. I wondered if the club bought its air fresheners from the same company that supplied the Cameo.

I found Piccolo polishing off a kid half his age in a squash match. At least I assumed he was polishing him off. Although I knew nothing about squash scoring, I jumped to my risky conclusion by the way the kid kept missing Piccolo's serves, by an inability to get his own past Piccolo, and, most of all, by the building resentment in the kid's eyes every time Piccolo barked out a number. The kid seemed to be as much of a bad loser at squash as Piccolo was in our fantasy baseball league.

The game finally ended, the kid managed a mechanical handshake, and Piccolo came through the door to the miniature theater protected by plexiglass where I was. "You're pretty good."

"I'm on the board," he said, unexpectedly gracious. "Only inferior players are admitted. What's so damn important it can't wait till Monday?"

"Joanna Mendler."

He didn't think that was worth even pausing in his toweling off. "The one from the movie house?"

"There may be some extra charges."

That did it for his graciousness, but he had to hold his fire as first the kid he had beaten passed through, then a well-built Asian entered for his turn on the court. "What the hell for?" he asked as the Asian began warming up.

"Record offices. They'll be closed on the weekend, but I can get somebody to open a few doors for a couple of bucks."

He was as incredulous as I figured he would be. "For this case of the century??!!"

"Sounds like you've been talking to Boardman. But I smell something here, Pete. No way a merry widow like Joanna Mendler should be making a stink about something like this. I've got a loose weekend. I'd like to put it together."

"Sure it's not too loose? Like maybe you'd like to make a mountain out of a molehill so you can climb the mountain?"

The trouble with that objection, of course, was that it might have been accurate. "You're the one who gave me the case."

He smirked, and I felt on the edge of getting a no. But then the door to the theater opened again, and the Asian's scheduled opponent entered. I told myself I was showing nothing as Robert Chichester, now in white togs and looking like swaddled roast beef, came flouncing down, exchanged greetings with Piccolo, nodded to me speculatively, and went out into the court.

"You know him?"

Piccolo shrugged. "Everybody in certain circles knows Chichester. Who'd you expect her to hire—some ambulance chaser from Queens?"

I didn't know what the coincidence meant, or even if it was a coincidence. All I kept thinking was that anybody else on the planet—George W. Bush, David Letterman, the prime minister of New Zealand—should have been flexing his fat arms out on the court, not Robert Chichester.

"Okay," Piccolo said, heading to the door. "But within limits, huh? And let's wrap it up fast. In case you've forgotten, we have more important things to do Monday."

"Right."

"Who gets top dollar this year?"

It took me a moment to realize he had stopped at the door and was waiting for a serious answer about our fantasy league draft Monday evening. "Rodriguez, Martinez, the usuals."

He nodded happily. "That's what I figured. Have a good weekend."

I looked back at Chichester's hippo form and knew I wasn't going to.

CHAPTER 10

I was right. Though I had patches of illusions otherwise.

Over a pizza at the kitchen table that night, I nimbly fielded the Professor's questions about Padres and Devil Rays he had never seen play or hadn't heard of period. My vanity got a charge every time he doublechecked on what I said with the *Sporting News Guide* and then docilely made a note on his yellow legal pad. I might have been the one who had to take notes when he went on about Joseph Needham's obsessive study of China or the cruel symmetries in the political careers of Cola di Rienzo and Aldo Moro, but he was the one who needed sharpened pencils for the previous year's developments at the Pittsburgh farm club in Oshkosh.

I was also feeling pretty good because I had finished transcribing my interview with Hammond the dentist and had found Patsy Bowes more than willing to accept a few dollars for some weekend overtime in the Mineola records office. Rookie shortstops, sadistic orthodontists, and clumsy widows—I had them all covered.

What I didn't have covered was Mary Reynolds.

It was almost ten o'clock when Gil Stedina called. He was an ex-cop from New York who had taken his pension, tried to make a go of it as a private investigator, then decided he stood a better chance for survival as a security guard waiting for burglar alarms to go off than as a gumshoe waiting for his telephone to ring. He was a member of our rotisserie league, and we got along well enough. When I heard his voice, I assumed he was just confirming our Monday night draft meeting. Wrong. What he was confirming was that Mary Reynolds was one of my clients. The same Mary Reynolds who had apparently burst into the video store at the mall to accuse one of the clerks there of knowing where her missing brother was. I had little choice but to leave the Professor to work out by himself the minor leaguers who might make the Brewers for the season.

Driving over to the mall, I wasn't my favorite person. For 48 hours or more, I had been slogging through the momentous affair of Joanna Mendler and the Cameo theater, while Tommy Reynolds had remained missing, if not arriving at an irrevocable stage of decomposition. What else could I have been doing to find him? I didn't know. Maybe there were a thousand avenues I had overlooked and I should have been concentrating on identifying them. What didn't seem to need any concentration was that spending time on Joanna Mendler was not one of the thousand avenues. Or so it seemed.

Because it was a Friday night, the mall was teeming with teenagers. Business looked particularly good around the two pizza stands and at a plastic attempt to reproduce an old-fashioned ice cream parlor. An Irish pub, on the other, was so darkly lighted it looked closed for the six or seven regulars stranded at the bar since lunchtime. Then there was Star Video, one of the last outposts against Netflix and which was booming even more than the pizza stands. There was barely enough room to squeeze through the aisles to the counter in the back. Even the curtained off porn section showed more shoes than a Florsheim's.

Mary Reynolds stood against the wall near the end of the counter. Stedina, next to her, wasn't restraining her with his hands, but he might as well have been. Mary seemed not even to recognize his presence. Her fearful, bloodshot eyes remained fixed on Richard Clary, one of the clerks I had interviewed on my first pass at the store. For his part, the Clary kid was dealing with a customer as nonchalantly as possible, leaving his third eye to vigilance over Mary.

She acknowledged my arrival with a nod, but without turning her head away from Clary. She wanted me to know at once why she was keeping her lips closed tightly. Before I could tell her I understood, the night manager Freed came out of the back room with a couple of movies for a waiting customer. As soon as he saw me, he forgot about the customer. "Thank you for coming," he said, sounding even noisier for his attempt at a whisper. "You must explain to Ms. Reynolds I'm as upset about Tommy as she is, but she can't just come in here and upset the store."

Mary finally blinked her way back into the people around her. "Richie knows where Tommy is, Mr. Finley," she said matter-of-factly.

Stedina had worked too many EDP cases in Manhattan for his own good; he seemed on the verge of pinning her arms back against the wall just for talking. I tried to be subtle about sliding between them. "I'll talk to him again, Mary. Now, why don't you go outside and wait for me?"

Freed was about to protest such a lenient solution, then registered the curiosity of some of the customers near the counter. He compromised by remembering he could get rid of at least one of them with the movies in his hand.

"Tell me, Richie!"

Stedina started to move in again at the shrillness in Mary's voice. Then the Clary kid decided he too had stood calmly too long. "Maybe if you'd lightened up on him," he said, a bitter glaze in his eyes, "he wouldn't have run off. You're not his mother."

I could have done without the venomous tone, but I didn't need Mary's lurch to get past me, either. I managed to grab one of her spindly arms before Stedina did. "All right, now get outside. You're not helping anything like this. Go ahead."

If I hadn't already realized how desperate she was, I would have gotten the message then and there: She was so reduced in her resources that I was all she had left. She nodded feebly and, not even bothering with a parting shot at Clary, marched her way through as many shoulders as she could hit on her way to the door. Stedina tried to recover some of his usefulness by trailing after her.

Freed finished recording his rental, waited till his customer had left, then turned to me with his arms extended in exasperation. "Think I don't feel for her? If it was my brother, I'd level the whole damn mall." He snapped back at Clary. "I don't want you holding back, Richie. You know something, tell them. I got a business to run here."

With that, Freed hustled back into the stock room and Clary looked after him as though he had lost an ally. I had seen a similar expression a hundred times in suspects who had just learned some confederate had rolled over on them. Or had I just seen fear before? "You're scared of something, Richie. What is it?"

Clary was as dark, angular, and pockmarked as Tommy Reynolds had been blond and chub-faced in his photographs. He looked at me as though I should have recognized the difference, grabbed a small pile of films, and went off after Freed to find their boxes.

Mary was sitting outside on the edge of a newspaper recycling crib. She was making a poor job of puffing on a cigarette. A band of teens loitered nearby with a proprietary air for having given her the cigarette. "Richie Clary knows where Tommy is, Mr. Finley," she said, preempting another lecture from me. "Those kids do, too."

"The cops questioned them all. I myself talked to Clary."

"You didn't do a complete job."

Criticism is always an opportunity for having second thoughts about the good qualities of the person leveling it. Clary had insinuated Mary was a Gorgon at home. I could see her being snippy, bitchy, and cold. But to the point of driving somebody out of the house and making him incommunicado? I couldn't buy it.

"You promised you were going to leave this to me."

She finally gave up faking her drags and tossed away the cigarette. "And is that what you, in turn, promised the police?"

"I haven't promised anybody anything, Mary. Any angle that occurs to me, with or without the cops, I'll pursue it."

She nodded; she didn't have much choice. But as she got to her feet, she finally asked the question I had been anticipating since seeing her state inside the store. "Do you know too, Mr. Finley? Do you know where Tommy is, too?"

I shook my head because that was what the puppet master pulling my strings told me to do.

"You know what I'm beginning to wish, Mr. Finley? I'm beginning to wish somebody would just come right out and say the worst so I wouldn't have to keep thinking it all by myself. When it's just me thinking it, it feels dirty—like I'm hoping for something instead of just thinking it."

I didn't dare take my eyes off her. "We'll find him, Mary. I'm going to go back over everything. I'll talk again to Clary and anybody else who ever knew Tommy. Okay?"

She had stopped listening at about the second word.

CHAPTER 11

I stayed up late that night watching television. For once, it didn't bother me they were reruns of shows I'd seen originally with Jennifer. I figured Tommy Reynolds might have seen them back then, too. I laughed a couple of times, even without nudging from the mechanical audiences.

CHAPTER 12

The next morning, I told myself I was still planning strategy for my next move in the Reynolds case while the Professor and I delved into whatever the county had on the Mendlers. Patsy Bowes, who had made every cop in Nassau grateful to her for showing them the hows and wheres of background research, sat near the door of the reading room alternately inventing tales about her nonexistent sex life or daring us to laugh at this or that admission she had none. I had warned the Professor not to go for the laugh. The one and only time I had fallen into Patsy's trap, she had instantly yanked a dossier out of my hand, told me she had had "more lovers than you've had wet dreams," and announced the office was closed. The Professor didn't raise his eyes to her once in two hours.

"Almost noon, Finley. Leave me some of my weekend, will you?"

"Almost there, Patsy."

Which would have been nowhere. Licenses, certificates, waivers—what they all added up to was that Joanna Mendler was rich because Harold Mendler had been rich and Harold Mendler had been rich because God, Allah, Buddha, and every mover and shaker on the east coast had insisted he be. There was real estate, there were banking and commercial interests, there were small fisheries, there were a hospital and a nursing home. More than that, there were letters of recommendation from people on Fifth Avenue and Wall Street that suggested an even bigger Harold Mendler beyond Nassau County.

What had I been looking for? Short of finding that Mendler owned the Cameo's block through some dummy corporation or that there was some blood tie between a Mendler and a Boardman, I didn't have the slightest idea. But somewhere in my visceral and calcium matter, I felt an old, unpleasant feeling—a feeling I had last had at St Theodore's Catholic Church the morning we had buried Jennifer and Susan. It was the feeling of *mockery*.

"Well?" Patsy sat slumped down with her arms folded across her chest. She must have been near retirement, but she hadn't looked all that much younger when I had needed her help for the first time 20 years before. Then she had had naughty eyes and short, straight black hair; now she had naughty eyes and short, straight gray hair.

"Ever go to the movies alone, Patsy?"

"Why should I? I'm always invited."

"Yeah, but what about that rare night when you've counted on staying home by yourself, then suddenly change your mind?"

She glanced up at the wall clock. "You're patronizing me, Finley."

"And I'm sorry. But I need your insight, love. I want you to pretend for one minute you once had a weekend when you had nobody around your finger and you ended up killing time by going to a movie alone."

She threaded and unthreaded her little fingers on the table in front of her. "Ask away. But my mind isn't part of the price. That's extra."

The Professor finally had to look up, and Patsy didn't appreciate it. He managed to get back to the ledger he was reading without betraying anything.

"Okay, picture it. A woman by herself. A rich woman. It's a Saturday night. Not to some superplex in a mall, but to a rathole joint that shows those martial arts things from Hong Kong."

"The Cameo?"

"Right. Tell me why she's there, Patsy."

"She likes kung-fu," she shrugged.

"Then she could rent the thing and have it on one of her 100-inch screens in her TV room or something. She could have the actors come over from Hong Kong and do it in her living room especially for her. But you know the Cameo. It gives you fleas just passing it on the street."

She finally seemed to think my question was serious. "Well, if she's not one of those masochists out for a thrill, it's got to be water."

"Water?"

"Her own, maybe. She had to go so bad she didn't mind paying for it. Or some louse made her cry and she wanted to hide it in the darkness, any darkness. Or it was raining and she didn't have an umbrella and didn't want to ruin her shoes. One kind of water or another."

I remembered what Mendler had said about her shoes during our interview. "Pumps."

"To get rid of the water?"

"No. What she was wearing."

Patsy didn't know what that clarified. She looked at the clock again. "You owe me extra for that insight," she said. "Could you shake your old friend there awake so we can get the hell out of here?"

The Professor shot his head up from the ledger. He wasn't in love.

CHAPTER 13

Levine came to the house that night to announce that Tommy Reynolds's body had been found in the woods near the old pond. I did the 10-minute drive behind him on automatic pilot. The most immediate task, I kept telling myself, was to fend off what Levine and Miles had in store for me. He hadn't liked being relegated to messenger and guide and figured to make up for it by asking—and asking again—why I had been so adamant about a banal missing person case. Ellen was his superior, but it was a homicide now, and she would give him some leeway.

Every time Mary Reynolds intruded on my thoughts, I dismissed her. She was for the distant future—in about an hour.

It was a full-dress Crime Scene in the woods. Every cop in the county seemed to have answered the call, bringing along with them every television station, newspaper, and supermarket handout in the Tristate area. There were about two dozen spectators idling near cars on the road. Even Robinson had been called in for cordon duty. I ignored his nod.

The body was covered by a police blanket at the edge of a clearing. Most of the technicals had come and gone, making me wonder how much debate had gone into the decision to fetch me. I didn't see the dog-walker who had apparently found the corpse, and toted that up as another sign of procrastination about coming for me.

Levine got his first orgasm by whipping the blanket off the body for maximum effect. It worked. The cleanest thing about what remained of Tommy Reynolds was his dirty blond hair. There were clots of dirt and leaves everywhere from his toes to his neck. The back of his head and neck were smeared with blood. If he hadn't been sodomized, he had been dropped ass-first onto a sharp rock.

"The whole schmeer," Levine volunteered in case I had gone blind. "Penetration. A hard implement to the skull. Could be a rock by the looks of it. I know a rock when I see it."

Especially when he held his brains up to a mirror, I thought and didn't say. Having passed the shock test, I turned away for a cigarette, only to realize I had left the pack home. Miles came out of the woods a few yards away. Had she been eavesdropping on me and Levine like some Shakespearian character hiding behind the drapes?

"Don't let his sister see him like that," I told her.

"You've seen worse," Levine said. "We all have."

I knew it was another test, but I didn't give a damn if I passed it or not. "His sister doesn't have to see him like that, you asshole!"

Levine smarted as though he had won at something. "Your ID isn't enough, Paul," Miles said. "You never met him."

I didn't wait for Levine to put a question mark on that observation. I headed back up to my car—toward the house for my cigarettes before I went to see Mary Reynolds.

"Your paperwork will be a help," Miles said, trudging after me. "Sure."

"And a statement about how you got involved and everything."

"It'll keep for a couple of hours."

"Don't go amateur on me, Finley." The authority of the investigating officer, and it wasn't me. "McGowan and a doctor are already on their way to see the sister."

I remembered the lush sitting at the corner desk in the bullpen. "You got to be kidding! What else you delegating to incompetents?"

"Pick up your notes and I'll meet you back at the office," she said evenly. "This isn't a wake, it's a homicide investigation."

I might have applauded her if I didn't feel more like throwing her back down the hill.

I was relieved, of course. The lush McGowan was going to have to handle Mary Reynolds's first reaction to the news, so I could wait until the following morning and drop in on her as just another mourner expressing his condolences. At least that was what I wanted to think as I returned home and went down to the basement to gather up everything I had on Tommy Reynolds. The Professor stood at the top of the staircase waiting for me to stop shoving everything but the stapler into my briefcase. "Can I say something?" he finally asked.

"No."

"He was already dead before the girl came to you."

"Been conducting your own investigation, Joe?"

"You know it as well as I do."

It was the wrong moment to glimpse the Niagara Falls photo. "Par for the course, then."

"You can't bring back the dead, Paul. I think it's worth saying."

"Okay, you've said it."

The red light was blinking on my answering machine. I assumed it had been blinking since I had walked in. I felt a chilly trickle in my intestines at the thought that Mary Reynolds had slammed the door in McGowan's face and run to the phone to tell me some creepy alcoholic cop was claiming Tommy was dead.

"Think things through. Maybe you *can* help Miles."

It was the Professor at his most irritating: the giver of exams first giving a pep talk to those about to reach for their pencils. I suddenly preferred even Mary Reynolds's crumbled innocence.

Except it wasn't Mary Reynolds on the machine.

"I hope I'm not disturbing you, Mr. Finley," Joanna Mendler purred. "But I didn't want you to draw any mistaken conclusions from our meeting. I'm sure you were puzzled I didn't have a crutch or cane with me. Aren't you paid for noticing such things? . . ."

"Turn that shit off!"

"The reason is very simple . . ."

The message ended abruptly. But I barely had time to register the Professor's rage before another one segued on.

"You should get a new machine. That tape is not very long. Anyway, the reason I didn't have my cane with me was that Mr. Chichester escorted me out to the patio before you arrived. So, no hasty conclusions. Thank you. Goodbye."

Had I needed that kind of pie in the face? I must have; even the Professor's fury didn't seem as convincing as he wanted it to be. "There's the kind of thing I can help with, Joe," I said, knowing I wasn't going to be contradicted. "I'm very good on cases like Joanna Mendler. Even she knows it. She's pissing her pants I caught her out. And know the funny thing? I hadn't even thought about a cane. I'd figured all along Chichester helped her out to the pool. So maybe I should even bear down a little more in my area of expertise. What do you think?"

He still hadn't answered by the time I got to the car with the Reynolds file.

CHAPTER 14

There were no pleasant surprises with Miles and Levine. As soon as we had finished going through my files, I graduated from helpful outsider to potential suspect; not a suspect exactly, just someone Levine wouldn't have minded seeing in that role. By the second pot he was even beginning to begrudge me the house coffee.

"All right," he said for about the fifth time, "this crowd at the mall where the kid hung out."

Sometimes Ellen stared at me for confirming consistency; other times she seemed adrift in her thoughts; still other times she seemed to be admiring Levine's relentlessness.

"Blank stares."

"So they knew something."

"They knew I was asking questions they didn't want to answer."

"Come on, Paul," Miles prodded. "Your gut."

"I've already given you that."

"Again. Please."

I agreed once more, and with the same rationalization for not telling them to go screw themselves—that maybe I would have recalled something for helping what was left of Mary Reynolds. "The kids are there every night, just hanging out. The video store where Tommy worked seems to be the center ring. This Clary kid, he works there, too. I'd focus on him for openers. Plus the list of customers." Miles still looked unenthusiastic about the customer's idea, and I still didn't know why. "I'm telling you, Ellen, if it was a pickup, the odds are it was somebody from the store. That means you start with the list of customers."

"That's a big mall. Even if we're talking about a pickup, it didn't have to be a video store customer."

"No, it doesn't. It might not even be anybody from planet Earth. But why not start with probabilities and work down to space creatures? It's the ideal setup. 'Hey, kid, have any special recommendations for me to watch tonight?'"

"They have homo pictures in their porn section?"

"I don't know, Herb. Check it out and get back to me."

"Okay, maybe the video store is the spot," Miles finally said with something like reasonableness.

I didn't wait for a second opening; it was near 11 o'clock. "Good," I said, grabbing my cigarettes and standing. "More than that I don't know."

Levine wasn't ready to be such a good sport. "Another few minutes, Finley. You know there's always something else."

I was saved from needing Ellen's mediation again by the arrival of half the mall at the entrance to the bullpen. The kids had been herded together by Lancaster and a couple of uniforms. I recognized Richie Clary and one of the kids who had given Mary Reynolds a cigarette.

"One of them Clary?" Miles asked lowly.

"The one with the bad acne."

"Okay. We'll take it from here."

For all his nervousness at having been hauled into a police station, Richie Clary still seemed to be toting some of the bitterness he had directed against Mary Reynolds. More than ever, his accusations seemed beside the point. "You convinced me, kid," I said to him. "Now I'm as scared as you are."

He looked right through me. That was a new development: Lately, I'd been feeling only transparent, not altogether invisible.

I lighted one cigarette too many outside the station house. I knew I couldn't go to bed without seeing Mary Reynolds, but I wanted the suddenly clammy air to give me an excuse not to. What it gave me instead was another reason to go: McGowan arriving and making a bad job of trying to walk soberly into the building. I didn't want to imagine how he had broken the news to Mary.

CHAPTER 15

I could have saved my dread going over to the Reynolds house. I hadn't counted on the Greggs, next-door neighbors who had insisted Mary spend the night with them after the doctor with McGowan had given her a shot. Old man Gregg was a retired fireman who thought he knew why I had come calling (a policeman) and why I couldn't postpone a look at Tommy's room (normal procedure). I didn't disabuse him of either notion; I was glad to get off his front stoop and over to the Reynolds house before Mary heard my voice in her sleep and woke up. As he opened the front door and turned on a light, Gregg kept reassuring me he and his wife had been "like grandparents" to Mary and Tommy all their lives. The only thing he seemed to disapprove of was the failure of the kids to attend Mass at Our Lady of Carmel with him and his wife on Sundays. "You wonder what state of grace he was in when this thing happened," he said to me, one Knights of Columbus member to another. "Of course that's nothing I'm going to say to Mary. You just have to trust it'll work out for Tommy."

Tommy's room was Classic Teenager. Walls plastered with rock group posters and school banners. A weight-lifting bench. CD player. Television. Computer. Low bookcase with what seemed to be mainly textbooks. A stack of videos. Magazines heavy on football and thong underwear. The doodads on the dresser and shelves were from a younger Tommy Reynolds—the one who had apparently liked sets. Flags of a couple of dozen nations. Terrible reproductions of Mets players on a plastic pedestal. Bears in tin, bears in iron, bears in ceramic. I could picture Mary feeding his attachment to bears so she would know what to buy him every birthday.

Gregg stood near the door monitoring my search. "The worst part will be when she wakes up. I don't know what we can say to her."

I made what I hoped was a sympathetic sound. What I wanted to know was whether McGowan had taken anything, but I let that lie until I could figure out a way of asking Gregg without arousing his suspicions about the communicating that went on down at the station.

I opened a dresser drawer and found a trove of condoms and swizzle sticks. "Oh, boy, that too?" Gregg asked, spotting the Trojans.

I threw the condoms back before he had a religious fit. I was more intrigued by the swizzle sticks. Most of them were from saloons out in the Hamptons and Montauk.

"One thing I got to say, the kid never gave me trouble. I guess most people would've expected it. You know, not having any parents around? But absolutely no trouble. I broke him in on my lawn. Saved me a lot of work . . . Is it a sex thing? That what you figure?"

"Could be." The second bureau drawer was all underwear, the third all neatly folded dress shirts and T-shirts. There was no way Tommy had been so meticulous. But then why had he gone out of his way to leave the condoms where Mary was sure to have spotted them? Had Richie Clary been getting at something specific at the video store with his outburst against her?

"We're really only neighbors. Mary could really use some family."

The bottom drawer was filled with more souvenirs from Montauk saloons—coasters, matchbooks, other swizzle sticks. I didn't know if the kid had been too young or too old to have such a trove, but I was sure it was one of them. "Mary and her brother go to Montauk much, Mr. Gregg?"

"Montauk? I don't think so. Sometimes she went off on Saturdays with Jerry Loeschen, the manager down at the grocery.

Nothing serious, you understand. The paper was always gone from her doorstep in the morning."

That sounded prudish even for him, and he started getting nervous. "What about Tommy?"

"Not that I know. He had school and his job at the video store."

"What about the weekends?"

He remembered he was supposed to be helpful. "Well, it's nothing I know for sure. But last summer he started not being around much on weekends. My wife asked Mary once. I think she just said Tommy was away with friends somewhere. If it's important, I can get my wife."

"It'll keep."

It was too much of a dismissive answer tied to the wrong move: He didn't like the way I pocketed some of the swizzle sticks. "The other one who was here, Sergeant McGowan, he wrote down whatever he took. For Mary, you know?"

I had no choice but to sit on the bed with my notepad to certify I was taking the stirrers. "What *did* McGowan take?" I asked, sounding tinny even to myself.

The answer was on a sheet of paper in the old man's pocket. "A class yearbook," he read. "Pay stubs from Star Video. A piece of rock."

I hadn't seen McGowan walking into the station house with any of those things. Had he just forgotten them in the car or exchanged them for a drink somewhere on the road? "What kind of rock?"

Gregg was back to looking grandfatherly. "Oh, it was an old thing I gave him. Came from Yellowstone Park when I was out there with Grace a few years ago. I don't know what McGowan would want it . . ."

I looked away before the tears exploded. I signed the note with my first name, middle name, and last name as he tried to catch himself. What the hell did McGowan think he had? The goddamn weapon used on the kid? Had Levine told him to look for a rock, any rock? And what about the computer? Had he bothered checking that out?

"What the hell's that?" Gregg was still wiping his nose, but his eyes were glued to the window. Either the sun had set a second time, and only a few blocks away, or there was a fire.

I shoved my receipt into the old man's hand and got to the small window before he could. The fire was a good half-mile away, but the glow in the sky dimmed every house light over to it.

"Where's that, Mr. Gregg?"

"The mall, I think."

I had a sinking feeling I knew exactly where in the mall.

CHAPTER 16

Trust your sinking feelings. When I finally got through the crawling, rubbernecking expressway traffic to the mall, I saw the video store was even a worse shambles than I had feared; about the only thing left to the place was its framework. The pizza stand next door was about to be stripped down to the same beams. I suppose it was the pizza association, but everything smelled like charred crust.

I spotted Miles conferring at the edge of the crowd of onlookers with a fire marshal and McDonough from the County Executive's office. I knew I was going to hear bad news even before I shouted to her over the cop who was trying to keep the curiosity seekers at bay. She confirmed my presentiment by sighing at the sight of me, then waving wearily to the cop to let me pass.

"You didn't get the customer files, did you?"

She tried to pretend she was surprised by the question. "That's just a theory."

"Pretty hot one, wouldn't you say?"

"Funny."

"What about Clary?"

She considered that more reasonable. "He could know something; he could be afraid of knowing something. We'll get it."

She looked back to where the firemen were flooding the pizzeria with their hoses, but where two huge jigsaw puzzle pieces of flame continued to dart in and out of the smoke. She was right, of course: Urgency had gone out the window the second Tommy

Reynolds's body had been found. Now there was just the slog of police work.

And if I had been Mary Reynolds, that wouldn't have satisfied me for a second. "Give, Ellen."

"Give what?"

"Just a fraction of what I've been giving you all night."

"Sounds like you're carrying more than a client on this."

"That should be enough. Between us, anyway."

She thought about it, then turned deliberately back to the fire. I had the feeling she didn't want anybody nearby overhearing her, or even reading her lips. "There's concern somewhere upstairs," the back of her head said. "Nothing I can put my finger on, but the video store's been mentioned." She shrugged. "Then again, I might be exaggerating."

I looked back at the firemen, too. What was the expression when you watched other people doing things you wouldn't have done even for a million bucks? "God, they've got a rough job!" Ellen's warning told me not to be so sure they did.

CHAPTER 17

I arrived in Montauk mid-morning Sunday. There was a smattering of activity around the coffee shops on the main street, and the sight of a couple of tall-masted boats returning to the harbor from an early excursion reassured me I wasn't the only one impatient for summer to begin. The 50-plus temperature helped, too. With a little imagination, I told myself, the morning might yet blossom into June, with droves of weekenders waiting on every corner to tell me what Tommy Reynolds had been up to during his weekend outings.

That fantasy lasted until I parked and began trudging around in search of the bars named on the swizzle sticks. Hard as it was to believe, Montauk saloons on Sunday mornings the first day of April cater only to upturned chairs, mops, and the overwhelming stench of detergent. Happy April Fool's Day.

But you take what you can get. The first place—the Caribbean—was stuck away in a dead end between the ocean and a bed and breakfast. The mop man didn't habla English, but the guy washing glasses behind the bar took a long, earnest look at one of Mary's photos (I had kept it because it showed an even younger Tommy Reynolds than the pictures I had given Miles). "Something about him," Helpful said. "Most of them, they look the same at that age, but I think I remember this kid. Too young even to try a phony ID, know what I mean?"

That seemed like enough bullshit for my first try, so I went on to Danny's in the main square. A birdlike redhead, sitting at a table near the door and flipping through the *News* comics, resisted even a look at the picture. "You're going to show me something sad, right? A kid that's dead or missing or something like that? I don't need that kind of downer so early in the morning."

"You'd be doing a lot of people a big favor."

Toll paid. She yanked the picture out of my hand and held it out at more or less the same distance she had been holding the comics. "Too young for here."

"Add a couple of years."

"Uh, oh. He's dead?"

"I didn't say that."

"No, you didn't. And that gets you a point. But I'll tell you, kids this age could turn into Russell Crowe or Alf two years later. What you got here isn't too helpful. Sixteen, seventeen now?"

"Right."

"You're in the wrong place. We do Yuppies, couples, that kind of thing. Nobody's paid for a meal in here with cash in years. And I don't have the patience for all that carding crap. You want the beer and barf joints. Try The Rook or Land's End."

I remembered both from the swizzle sticks. "Thanks."

She held on to the picture another second. "Is the kid from out of state?"

"No. Why?"

"Nothing special," she said, thinking better of something and yielding the photo. "You're from out of state, it can be any port in a storm, that kind of thing."

"I don't think I'm following you, Mrs. . . . ."

She glanced over to where her small daughter was making a mess out of trying to sweep under a table with a broom twice her size. "They call me Hilary. Danny the owner's my father. It's just that some of the kids, especially during the summer, they come out and end up doing anything for a laugh. Right?"

"I don't know."

She was getting impatient with my thickness. "You know—drugs, drinking."

"Yeah, I've heard of them. Goes on everywhere."

"Yeah, kids are kids." She suddenly preferred looking down at *Hagar the Horrible*. "When I was a kid and hung out with kids, I did the same shit. I'm not a kid anymore, so I don't hang around with kids. But not everybody has those prejudices."

It was the pickup theory again. "This place, The Rook . . ."

"No, no," she said quickly. "Billy Holland may not mind wiping up puke, but he runs a straight place. Let's just say the invitations were already in the mail."

We *could* have said that if I'd understood what the hell she was talking about. But I didn't, and Hilary was at the end of being cooperative. Anything else, she said under a shout to her daughter to take the broom outside, would have been mere "gossip."

I hit the street again thinking of every possible variation—dirty old men, dirty old women, rich old men, rich old women, not so old dirty, rich men, not so old dirty, rich women. But the picture of Tommy Reynolds trying to blackmail some score and getting cracked over the skull for his enterprise just didn't fit into the bedroom I had looked over. Nothing whatsoever in that room had suggested the risk attached to any extortion scheme.

I had to ask three people for directions to The Rook. The most helpful was the third, a cab driver who pointed two doors down from where we were standing on the avenue and insinuated I needed tests from the optometrist or brain surgeon of my choice. Then I saw a mirage, on a terrace cafe hanging over the street. There was room only for a half-dozen tables on the terrace. Divide that into the population of Long Island, New York, and the Tristate area, and even without counting the rest of the country and planet, the odds should have been steep against one of those six tables being occupied by Joanna Mendler and Robert Chichester. I suddenly had an alarming clue as to why people kept playing the state lottery.

CHAPTER 18

She was delighted to see me, he wasn't. She couldn't ask enough questions about my reasons for being in Montauk and then about the Reynolds case, he couldn't sort out his *Times* sections loudly enough to show me how he had been counting on spending brunch. In the third corner was the gibbering idiot. Was I supposed to assume she and Chichester were an item? Should I have been careful not to betray a hint of disappointment at her taste? Why did her long, elegant body look like it was slumming in the world of cloth? I had twice as many questions as she had.

"That sounds horrible," she said when I finally ran out of breath. "But I suppose you must be used to more than injury claims."

"I hope not."

It came out too heavily, and she looked genuinely embarrassed as she retreated to her coffee. I said the first thing that occurred to me. "But I appreciated your message."

Lies are supposed to have a purpose; this one didn't. Chichester glared at her. Now she looked embarrassed from both ends of the table. "I hope it tied up any loose ends," she managed.

"Just about."

"Then you're finished your report?"

"Just about."

Chichester had enough of the Style section. "I don't think this is a proper line of conversation, Joanna. After all, Mr. Finley represents Gramercy's interests."

"Nonsense. Mr. Finley isn't hiding a mike, are you?"

I was beginning to think I was always going to need Chichester with her; he seemed to bring out her gamesmanship. "No mike."

"Well, we're running behind, anyway," he said, consulting what looked like the priciest of TAG Heuers. "They're waiting for us."

"Softball," she explained to me. "A ritual Robert has dragged me into. The lawyers against the insurance men."

"Early in the season for that, isn't it?"

Chichester slipped some bills under the check; he looked annoyed by her sudden detachment from their plans. "It isn't the lawyers against the insurance men," he said emphatically. "It's between the people who visit during the summer and the year-rounds. We've been doing it for years."

"It still isn't summer."

He finally had to acknowledge me as more than the thing sitting to the left of his friend. "Opening Day is Tuesday. We have this ritual game the Sunday before Opening Day. Kind of like our spring training. We don't really start the league games until after Decoration Day."

For all his pompousness, Chichester couldn't disguise the zealot's passion. I figured him for the catcher—or a stroke.

"Do you play, Mr. Finley?" she asked from a new level of coy.

"Only on paper. We have this rotisserie league . . ."

"Oh, where you all sit around and bid on these phantom players?"

"The players aren't the phantoms. The idea of owning them is."

It was my first shot of the morning, and she appreciated it. He didn't. "Not very much exercise that way," he snapped, making a project of getting his heft out from under the tiny table. "Should find some friends and have regular games, Finley. I'm sure you can find someplace to play in Garden City."

She watched me for a reaction. As Piccolo had said, she hadn't hired an ambulance chaser from Queens: She *expected* her employees to have the last word. "When I do, Bob, can I put you on the roster?"

It wasn't much, but it helped her make up her mind. "I have an idea. Why don't you come with us? These bartenders you have to talk to won't be on duty until this afternoon at the earliest."

"Joanna, you know how they are . . ."

She had heard enough from the privy council. "You're one person short anyway, Robert. I can't play with this leg. Mr. Finley can be my . . . What do you call it? My pinch-hitter?"

"Replacement. A pinch-hitter replaces somebody during a game."

"Oh."

Which was what Chichester was thinking as he studied her for some sign she wouldn't insist on my coming along. He had to settle for the consolation prize of helping her to her feet and then providing his shoulder for the walk downstairs to his car. I told myself I wouldn't have proposed brunch at the top of a staircase to somebody with a gimpy leg, especially one who was once again without her cane.

She extended her leg in the back seat of Chichester's Lincoln while I sat up front. The five-minute ride to the softball field was taken up with her monologue on the people I would be playing with and against. "Willy Baker and his wife Cecile, they're the ones you want to be nice to. The story is that Willy's maternal grandfather wasn't satisfied bilking gold and silver investors in Manhattan. He also came up with some scheme to cheat all his friends in the Hamptons. For the first and last time in history, all the Hamptons came together for the purpose of freezing him out of their circle. By way of revenge, he set himself up in some monstrous castle in the Hither Hills and every morning went down to Napeague Bay with his nets to gather up all the old hundred-dollar bills the Hamptons swells had flushed down the toilet the night before. Before you knew it, he'd dried out enough bills to be as wealthy as they were. Willy's mother and father tripled that in the stock market, and Willy himself is now in the first of his thousand lives for spending what he's inherited. If you ever want to enlarge your company, Mr. Finley, Willy's the one to talk to."

Chichester did a good job of keeping his eyes on the road.

CHAPTER 19

The softball field was as advertised—a couple of dozen middle-aged people in spotless Dockers and tailored jeans throwing balls around and not looking especially nimble at it. Chichester got two gloves out of his trunk and tossed me one at the speed Japanese hitmen fire their lethal stars. Joanna seemed to think I had lost a point with that gesture, so she restored the balance by grabbing my arm after lifting herself out of the back seat. "Deposit me close, but not too close," she ordered.

I headed toward a patch of dead grass midway between home and first. I sensed every eye on the field on us, and decided she did, too, and that was why she was hopping twice as severely as she had been leaving the cafe with Chichester. I kept a stupid smile plastered on my face for one and all. I was so busy liking that pose that it wasn't until I lowered her on the ground that I realized my loafers and corduroys weren't the ideal togs for hustling around the bases after my 600-foot drives.

"They can be your excuse when you make an error," she offered.

"Maybe I won't make an error."

"That would be different."

It wasn't just Chichester I needed in her company, I thought, I also could have used a Bada-Boom drum.

"Looking for rotisserie recruits, Finley?"

It was my second mirage of the day. Piccolo couldn't have smirked more at my surprise.

"Hello, Pete," she said.

"Joanna."

My first reaction, of course, was to think of all the reasons it should not have been a surprise to have Pete Piccolo standing five feet in front of me. He knew Chichester. He had alluded to his weekends "at the end of the Island" more than once over the years. And his look of having been caught at something as much as doing the catching, well, that, I told myself, was because he had never counted on my seeing him in his Yale sweatsuit.

I bought all those reasons for about five seconds.

"On the other team now, Paul?"

"I've been drafted."

"Mr. Finley's our secret weapon," she said, not all that cordially.

Piccolo seemed to think that was funny, then gave a little wave and trudged off toward home plate. She stared after him angrily, and I assumed I knew why. "It's still Sunday, it's still softball, and we don't have to think of the Cameo today," I said.

She nodded pensively, then came back to me. "You didn't know he comes out here a lot?"

"Lots of things I don't seem to know."

"Well, I'm going to take you at your word," she said, reaching into her bag for a cigarette. "Today you're with Robert against Pete Piccolo, and we won't think of other things. Agreed?"

What else was there to do *but* agree?

PLAY BALL!

I needn't have worried about ruining my loafers running out titanic home runs. A strikeout, a popup to the pitcher, and a popup to the shortstop make for little wear on shoe leather. I'd also exaggerated the dangers to my shoes from pursuing line drives to the center fielder, since Willy Baker, grandson of one of the Island's original financial marauders and captain of the home team, took one look at me and pronounced me best suited for the position of catcher. That would have been a compliment in the National League, but on Hither Field it meant I stood a couple of feet behind batters who swung at every pitch they saw. I caught as many useless relay throws from infielders as soft-toss deliveries from Willy.

I was also wrong about Chichester. He might have looked like the average wallowing mammoth, but he could hit, and was no embarrassment at first base. For eight innings, he seemed to do nothing but chug out extra-base hits, dig bad throws out of the dirt, wipe his shirt over the Niagara of sweat gushing down his face, and leer at me for my hasty expectations. I consoled myself with two thoughts: Joanna was *really* going to have to favor me if she wanted to restore the balance between me and Chichester, and the elephant might still have his stroke.

Despite my contributions, Chichester's team was leading 7-6 in the ninth inning. Most of the spectators (who included locals who had shared in the looting of a store that sold lumberjack shirts and Navy baseball caps) thought that was only right since the weekenders had already taken away too much of their space. Piccolo's teammates didn't seem to care all that much, either: They were having fun and the game marked their Groundhog Day for the pleasant weather to come. A woman named Marge kept crying "Win or Lose—Play with Style!" and that seemed to be the general mood.

Except for Piccolo.

Pete Piccolo didn't like to lose—Gramercy insurance money, alimony hearings, or fantasy league stakes. He didn't like losing meaningless softball games, either. When I could forget about Chichester's leers, I could see the tension building in him from the moment our team took a three-run lead in the sixth inning. Every time Marge let loose with one of her good sportsmanship cries, he seemed to contemplate another use for his bat. It didn't help, either, that his two errors at third base had helped to manufacture our lead. By the ninth inning his black eyes had pierced through all the hoi polloi around him and received the vision: He had no teammates and no opponents, but only himself and his powers for correcting the universe.

Naturally, I tried to make him feel worse when he came to bat as his team's last hope. "Easy out, Willy!" I yelled out to Baker. "The easiest out of all!"

I can appreciate a comeback as much as anyone. What I wasn't expecting was that it would be: "Found a new line of work?"

I started to laugh, but then his leaden tone settled down on my ear. He kept waving his bat at Baker—not minimally interested in reassuring me that a crack was only a crack.

Nicely for vengeful events, Baker's first pitch sailed in a foot too high and Piccolo swung at it wildly. Even better, I caught the damn thing. That made me benevolent enough to say: "Loosen up, Pete. It's a goddamn game."

He stepped back from the plate, ostensibly for a better look at the outfield arrangement. I thought that was precious of him since all his hits had been 100-foot humpbacks over the heads of the infielders. "You start diddling around with the claimant," he muttered, "I think that's what they call a conflict of interest, isn't it?"

I looked over to where Joanna was sitting on the grass. A redheaded girl no more than four or five was parked between her legs and clapping for Baker on Joanna's lead. The sight of the two of them drained the last reserves of hale fellowship I felt toward Piccolo. "That seems to be your specialty, too. Or did it just slip your mind you knew everybody?"

He got back into the batter's box. "I'm not filing the preliminary report, you are."

I didn't know what that answered. Baker's next toss was even more exquisite—an outside dip that had Piccolo grunting futilely after it like an inept golfer. "Fucking great game, ain't it, Pete?"

He was being a bad sport, and I was being a bad sport. The difference, I wanted to believe, was that he was a wannabe jock who saw his balls on the line every time he laced up his Pumas, while I was an investigator who wouldn't have minded having one less file from Gramercy Insurance. There was no reason to think Piccolo would use that as an excuse to drop me altogether, right? At the very least, it would make things awkward at our fantasy draft session Monday night.

Baker released his third toss, and as I watched it come, panic set in. I had just screwed up everything! The Mendler case, my work with Gramercy, even our damn rotisserie league! Was I out of my fucking mind!

And then Piccolo cracked the hardest hit ball of the game.

It started out as a laser beam over the shortstop's head, then seemed to pick up speed as it cut the grassy dirt between the center and left fielders. A moan went up from the locals, while Marge and the rest of Piccolo's teammates came alive in unison off their bench, screaming him on. As I watched the two outfielders chase after the ball, I put Marge down as a hypocrite: She hadn't been satisfied just playing, after all.

The ball might have kept going to the Atlantic if Mars or one of the other all-time all-star deities hadn't intervened. But intervene it did, in the form of a wheelbarrow that had been left in the far reaches of the field. The ball hit the wheelbarrow so hard it took a violent carom up into the air. By the time it came down, the left fielder, a publishing guy named Fred, was there to grab it, whirl, and fire back to the infield. A sure home run had been kept to a triple.

I thought.

Piccolo had barely arrived at third base when the shortstop had Fred's relay and turned to find me. I didn't want to be found. Run in the ball, I wanted to scream. Don't make a wild throw. Don't give away what they can't take. Don't throw me a bomb and have me let it get through. You've ignored me for 8 2/3 innings, ignore me a little more.

The shortstop, some kind of investment counselor named Robin, had no choice. Piccolo took it away from him as soon as he reached third, rounded it, and kept coming. I knew nothing good was going to happen as I kicked the bat out of the way and bent over in my best imitation of a catcher about to get killed. Robin had an accurate arm. The ball came on a single, neat bounce; the little redhead sitting with Joanna wouldn't have missed it. I double-clutched to be sure, and that was almost my undoing. In the fraction of a second that I slapped my free hand over the ball in my mitt, I caught those black eyes again. They were at the top of a Yale locomotive that had no intention of sliding; it was coming straight for me. I wasn't a catcher anymore. I was a Nassau County cop steeling myself for firing my weapon. I saw the perp, saw his elbows go up, saw the vulnerable chest he had left for me. He didn't see what I had seen, and he didn't see my left knee, either. It was one bulwark more than I had counted on.

The left elbow hit me above my right ear. I knew that was going to hurt a second or a year later, but I still had that interval for slapping my mitt, my irritation with bad sports, and all the money I had lost in our fantasy league into the big Y emblem for Yale. Piccolo was at the end of all the shoves, and looked astonished to be. His mouth opened as he staggered back and then fell. His body must have hit a button in the ground because, suddenly, the screaming at me that had been going on everywhere around me changed very clearly into screaming *for* me. I heard it, I relished it, I thought sure Joanna and the little girl were the loudest voices of all. Not even my throbbing ear counted.

Then Piccolo spoiled it all. He was winded and disgusted. He couldn't manage to lift his eyes from the ground to my face to say something like "Good block, Paul babe." But he did manage to raise his look as far as my left knee—where, I saw, he had ripped a hole in my pants big enough to fit my catcher's mitt.

CHAPTER 20

As Mike Piazza could attest, every good play at the plate unleashes the freebies. Willy Baker decreed that I deserved the game ball. His wife Cecile made sure I got the first beer from her cooler. My good pal Bob Chichester couldn't pound me enough on the back. More important, he was the first to insist I join everyone at the "Spring Training Party" the Bakers were hosting later in the day. And when he realized the shape I was in, he couldn't be talked out of driving me over to what he called his "shack" for a shower and change of clothes. Joanna's merry smile said she wouldn't have it any other way.

The "shack" had never been home to moonshiners. It was a reconverted bungalow of four or five spacious rooms about 100 yards off the ocean. It might not have been an ideal hideout for hurricanes, but otherwise seemed perfectly suitable for weekend retreats by a president of the United States. The only thing missing from the burnished wood paneling, cushion-plump divans, and fireplace in the main room was a marlin or two fixed to a plaque. Clearly, my good pal Bob Chichester didn't waste his time with the Atlantic seaboard's smaller fish.

My shower would have been nicer if I didn't waste so much of it concluding that Chichester's invitation had also been aimed at letting me see where he and Joanna got away from it all. That in turn made me annoyed to think I had developed a good-sized case of coveting my neighbor's fortune. Even a couple of days before, I might have been satisfied to rationalize that my Id had not only come awake, it was bent on sweeping across the plains like Attila the Hun. I made a mental note to ask the Professor how Attila had gotten his in the end.

When Chichester had mentioned he could find some clothes to replace my ripped pants and *eau de nature* shirt, I had imagined an outfit that would allow me to attend the party as Bozo the clown. Instead, when I stepped out of the shower, I found a perfectly fitting pair of jeans and black shirt. Apparently, his previous guests had been Tony Camerino and the boys from the Rockaway Social Club. I didn't dwell on why Tony didn't need his shirt anymore.

I found Joanna in the main room mixing gin and tonics at the bar. She had changed into a silver pants suit and had the gleam of having stepped out of her own shower. My cunning deduction was that she and Chichester had more private waters in another corner of the shack.

"They'll do," she said, studying my attire.

I didn't hear anybody moving around in other rooms. "Where's Chichester?"

"He went ahead to the party. Robert could win a landmark appeal before the Supreme Court and never mention it. But win a softball game? He'd call a press conference to gloat. Hope this is okay for you."

The limp was back as she came out from behind the bar with the drinks. The postgame beer had been enough for me for the moment, but I didn't want her feeling unappreciated, either, so I took a sip. "How many places like this does he have around the world?"

"Just this one and his house," she said, getting down on a divan near the cigarettes she had left on the table. "And the answer to your question is, no, we're not. Robert likes women as his best friends. It's very trendy with some men these days."

That should have amounted to another perfect block at home plate for me. But with the opposition out of the way, the repartee had also lost its flavor. "When do you stop?"

"Stop?"

"Saying smartass things."

She took a strand of tobacco off her lower lip only to gain time for something else. It wasn't anything I might have expected. "There's something you should know," she said. "When you gave Piccolo that shove before, I suddenly lost my interest in this other business. I've already told Robert."

"All this was just so you could stick it to Piccolo??!!"

"Gramercy's his company. He likes to lose even less than Robert."

An old desk sergeant named Jerry Cohen once told me every important lie comes wrapped inside a distracting fact. The distracting fact, I decided, was Pete Piccolo's passion for trampling over old ladies if they stood in his way. "Bullshit."

She seemed to consider that reasonable as I sat down next to her; she smelled off-orange, more orangeade than whole pulp. "When my husband died a couple of years ago," she said after a moment, "Piccolo was like one of those TV ads. Take the widow's hand at the cemetery and assure her he'd do everything to help he could. Ten months later, the bastard finally authorized payment on the policies."

I didn't know what to say. The Piccolo I had met after Jennifer's accident had been just the opposite. But that had also been before the divorce that had soured him on the world. "You're serious, aren't you?"

"Very," she said evenly.

"What happened to your husband?"

"I'm sure you've looked that up."

Of course I had when I had been investigating her. How had I managed to erect that separating wall without my brain noticing? "Cancer."

"A very long one. There's always somebody at a funeral who'll say maybe it's for the best. This time he was right. Piccolo, though, wanted to drag it out even longer. I guess Gramercy really needed the bank interest building up on the indemnity."

"Just that?"

She took a long swallow. Her throat was as composed as the rest of her—no unnecessary ripples. "You're an investigator," she said. "You have to look into why sleazy things happen. I'm not that curious. I just try to make them sorry they happened to me."

I held her gaze for a second more than I had intended or she had counted on. It wasn't a full plunge, but it stabbed hotly enough.

She put down her glass and stood up. "Let's go to Willy's."

"I came out here for a reason. Maybe you could drop me off at my car, I could see this guy at The Rook, then catch up to you at the party."

"Would you really come?"

"I said I would."

"I'll ask again: Would you really come?"

"With my gigolo shirt on? I don't dare be seen in Garden City in this. I'll come back later and get my stuff."

"Okay."

She made it sound like a compromise in which she had given up more than she had gained. She made up for that as soon as we arrived back in the center of Montauk. "The Rook is two blocks down there," she said, pulling in next to my car and reminding me where the cab driver had pointed. "Mind if I tag along? I've never seen a detective at work."

"Investigator. Detectives detect. I just investigate."

"I've never seen much of that, either."

With her claim against Gramercy out of the way, she had only the slightest of hitches as she held my arm down to The Rook. There were a lot more people on the street now, and I would have bet most of them had come to see the guy who had blocked home plate, wore the shirts of cheap gunsels, and led the most beautiful woman on the Island to saloons. Of course, no fashion magazine would have called her the most beautiful. Her face was too spare, her eyes held out the possibility she would settle for the artificial if it was amusing enough, her suit smoothed out one softness too many from those I recalled from her bathing suit. But I preferred the Finley Test to the standards of any fashion magazine: When other women passed us, they sneaked annoyed, critical looks at her. I've never known the Finley Test to fail.

The Rook was midway between a sports bar and an off-campus hangout. Three TV sets had college basketball games going—the University of Wyoming Agricultural Manure against the University of North Carolina Recruitment Violation or something. This seemed thrilling enough for the young 20's clustered around the bar or sending up periodic cheers from the tables. It dawned on me that even this crowd was much too old for Tommy Reynolds.

The only thing I discovered from the owner Billy Holland was that he was hung up on the handlebar mustaches and slicked-down hair of barbershop quartets. A baldheaded bartender named Archie studied my photograph a long moment, nodded that Tommy Reynolds might have been a kid he had refused to serve a few months ago, then gave me back the picture with a shrug of so what. The light at the end of my tunnel blinked a couple of times, then went out. Archie was absolutely right: *So what?* I had succeeded—maybe—in tracing Tommy Reynolds to a Montauk tavern where he hadn't been served. That piece of trivia might have been more novel than flowers, but it didn't figure to console Mary Reynolds much at the funeral.

"You don't remember if he was with somebody, do you?" I asked, mainly to postpone having to walk out the door again.

Archie looked like he had been asked to guess the weight of the solar system. "Hey, I'm talking a while back," he protested over another roar for a basket.

"Well, when you didn't serve him, did he just leave or did he hang around? Maybe sit at a table and wait for somebody else to buy him?"

Archie was a good sport, even with an obnoxious jock from the other end of the bar slamming down his glass and demanding another beer. "They're always trying to get somebody else . . . No, wait a minute. I remember. He went back to that table over there. There was another kid with him. In fact, . . . let me see that again."

I had nothing to lose. Maybe he was bullshitting me like the first guy at the Caribbean, maybe not. Joanna stood near the door as though watching brain surgery from as close as she wanted to be.

"No," Archie said. "This kid here, he was the one sitting over at the table. It was another one who asked me for the beers. When I said no to the beers, this one got up from the table and said he wanted a Coke. That's why I remember him standing here."

"The one who asked for the beers—what did he look like?"

"Bad face," he said immediately. "Lot of Clearasil in Mom's medicine cabinet."

At bottom, it was another So What. Richie Clary had never denied being a friend of Tommy Reynolds. But it still felt like a better So What than the others I had collected.

CHAPTER 21

We took my car over to the Bakers if only to give me something to do besides stare into space and pout. Still trying to act impressed by my adventurous way of making a living, Joanna asked to see the photograph. "There must be a hundred kids out here that look like this," she said.

"Not to their mothers and fathers."

"I've probably seen him myself."

"Wouldn't surprise me."

"What do you mean by that?"

I hadn't meant anything, certainly nothing calling for the sudden hurt in her eyes. *Had* I? "The convergence of things."

"What's that?"

"Well, just coming out here on this case and finding you. Then you and Piccolo. All these coincidences. Why not a couple more? A famous man once said luck was the residue of design."

"Coincidence isn't luck."

"It is if you're an investigator stumbling across the coincidences."

She relented if only to point me up a hilly road. "I see," she said frostily. "So you're a living example of Pasteur's dictum."

"What Pasteur? It was Branch Rickey who said that luck was the residue of design."

"That baseball person? Well, that may be. But your Mr. Rickey was plagiarizing Louis Pasteur. The exact quote is, 'Chance favors only the prepared mind.'"

There was a curve on the road, and another one inside the car. "Where'd you pick that up?"

She had regained some high ground and smiled to see I recognized it. "Oh, you mean where did the bimbo find time to read about Pasteur while she was so busy sunning herself at the pool, getting her skin peeled, and counting her old husband's millions?"

It was too late to retreat. "Something like that."

She decided I deserved a reward. "I know a great deal about 19th-century French history. I studied it at Temple, worked at the French Academy for three years, and, believe it or not, usually know the French words in the *Times* crossword puzzle."

I was humiliated enough not even to say *touché.*

CHAPTER 22

The Baker estate wanted to look like a lot of things—a carriage house magnified ten times over, a museum of mobile human beings, the most opulent military barracks ever conceived. But whatever the day-to-day whims of its drunken architect, it had maintained its central motif of What Do I Do with My Money. If Joanna's tale about Baker's grandfather had any truth to it, she had left out the part where the alienated Hamptonites had sneaked onto the grounds every night to titter at the *nouveau riche* monstrosity that sought to be superior to their digs.

The ground floor leaned heavily toward the museum inspiration, consisting of a series of arched halls where even the warehouses of furniture dumped into the rooms looked like miniatures. The custodian was Baker himself, who came spinning across the marble floor as if someone had pushed him and he couldn't stop. He had traded in his T-shirt and Pumas for a green silk shirt that might have been the envy of most mirrors.

"I was wondering where our defensive star was! By now Fred's telling everybody it was his pickup that won the game and Robin's bragging only his relay made it possible. Another few minutes, and they would've forgotten you were even in the game!"

Baker had a point. The publishing guy Fred and the shortstop Robin had half a dozen people cornered as they pantomimed the action of the last play. Something told me right away that, for more than reasons of boredom, I shouldn't have been interested in them.

"As for Bob, if he tells one more person how he might've been a big-league prospect, he's going to turn into a baseball!"

Across the ballroom from Fred and Robin, my good pal Bob Chichester looked three sheets to the wind as he yammered on to another small group. The ferret suddenly working on my nerves said he wasn't what I should have been concentrating on, either. I felt warmer at the sight of the small bandstand at the back of the room. The musicians were all dressed in the kind of bolero outfits favored by Rudolph Valentino and Diego of the Sunrise Highway Lounge. They were grinding through a thrombic version of some 1970s song I usually listened to with half an ear on the car radio. There were two saxophonists, two guitarists, a drummer, and a keyboard player. One of the sax players and one of the guitarists were women.

The ferret bit hard. No, they weren't women, I saw again; they were girls. And the males were decidedly high school boys. And on to the waiters who were circulating in the same bolero gear: They too still seemed to have college in their future.

A dozen or more Tommy Reynoldses.

I looked back at Joanna in astonishment. I didn't know exactly what I wanted to accuse her of, but I knew I had to have a better explanation of our little conversation in the car about coincidences. She wasn't there for my demands. Cecile Baker had joined us, and she had kisses for everybody, even me.

"Next year we're going to do this in a locker room," she gushed. "Well, you look like you've recovered from your collision. Nice shirt."

Joanna's expression seemed to mean I should smile at Cecile. I smiled at Cecile.

"The bars are over there," she said, pointing out two long tables against a far wall. "Get yourself something while I steal Joanna a minute."

I had a feeling Cecile had forgotten my name, and was whisking Joanna off to be told again what it was. Everything was suddenly grist for my mill. If the Bolsheviks had been outside the door, I would have gone over to let them in. Instead, I settled for a ginger ale at the bar. A tall scarecrow with an ill-fitting rug watched me watching the kid behind the bar pour the soda. I hadn't remembered him from the game. "You AA?" he suddenly piped up.

There were two ways to go, but one might have endangered Tony Camerino's shirt, so I took the other. "No, it's Finley, Paul Finley."

Scarecrow seemed reluctant about shaking hands. "I just assumed . . ."

"Yeah, well," I said magnificently, dropping a buck in the kid's plate. "You never know what people are off these days. So much to kick and so little time to do it in."

I had wanted to talk up the bartender, but Scarecrow showed no intention of moving. I had little choice but to circulate and catch one of the waiters for my questions. For somebody who had been Julius Caesar reentering Rome only a couple of hours earlier, I had little trouble navigating around by myself. The few eyes that looked up at me placed me or didn't, then dropped back to their more immediate entertainments. Every other conversation centered around the kind of rotisserie league Piccolo and I had put together. Some of the guests had their own league drafts scheduled for the following night, some had already held them the night before. The names Rodriguez, Jeter, and Hunter rolled around the room the way IBM and GE had in a more innocent age. I didn't know if I was getting sick of baseball or of my fantasy role in it. Or was it just that the swells around me were a reminder that even the same fantasies weren't always equal?

"You owe me, brother!"

Marge, the sport of sports who had shown her true colors in screaming on Piccolo, slid between me and the waitress I had been aiming for. She was a wiry blonde with a raspy voice, probably not 40. She also seemed to be the only one in the room who had come directly from the field: She still wore her Mets cap and Columbia sweatshirt. In the interests of getting my mouth moving, I pointed out that uniqueness to her.

"You mean I stink?"

"I mean you smell like roses. When you're not being a hypocrite on the field, anyway."

I didn't know what I was talking about, and she certainly didn't, but that suddenly seemed fine. We both decided we had met in another life before there had been any Bakers to host us. But she didn't tell me anything useful, either.

"You always ask so many questions, Finley?" she said finally. "Don't get me wrong. I don't mind questions. I assume you want to invest with a trustworthy broker. But you're not asking the right questions."

She gave me another hoarse laugh and sipped more scotch. I laughed at the thought that I had fallen into another ditch: Only somebody *very* close to the Bakers wouldn't have hesitated to show up in her Mets cap and Columbia shirt. Did she even live in Xanadu?

She didn't give me the chance to add still that question, flagging down Cecile for something about a sculpture show. At least I didn't have to lick that wound. The sight of one of the waiters—nametag KEVIN—heading for the kitchen for more shrimp rolls got me back to the only questions I wanted to ask. "Mind telling me who the caterer is?"

KEVIN probably centered the ball for his high school team. Everything about him was thick. "Excuse me?"

"I was thinking of having a party myself. Just wondering what outfit you guys worked for."

"Oh. Well, the food I don't know. I just answered an ad."

"In the paper?"

"No, no. Gloria and I . . . That's her over there." He nodded to a dark, petite waitress who was serving the Fred-Robin circle. "We saw it in Video Views."

The ferret was back, and this time it was gnawing at some basic circuitry. "Video Views?"

"Video place in Babylon. That's where we live. I'm going inside for more shrimp if you want any."

I thanked him, and he went off to the kitchen with his empty tray. Did I really have a piece of hard information? Had the real cause of the fire at Star Video been the ads tacked on the bulletin board? That didn't make sense. Even if somebody didn't want the ads to be seen, how hard would it have been just to rip them off instead of starting a fire that might have killed somebody?

"You look recovered."

So did Piccolo. He looked almost human in his creased slacks and white sports shirt; there was even a hint of a smile. "If you'd slid, you might have been safe."

"And break my ankle? Forget it. Let me buy you a drink."

I got a Tom Collins to celebrate my half-fact from KEVIN. Piccolo wasted whole seconds before he nodded over to Joanna. "She tell you she changed her mind?"

"That why you're having an attack of pleasant?"

"C'mon, you've seen Boardman's operation. I've been recommending dropping the place for years. Star Video may need it for taxes or whatever, but Gramercy doesn't."

"Excuse me?"

"The people who own Star Video," he said innocently. "They own the Cameo, too. I bet some of them are in this room. I know they are."

The room started to spin; ever so perceptibly, but spin nevertheless. "Like who, for example?"

He was delighted by my expression. "You want to look up cousins of second cousins, go ahead. Gramercy went as far as the official owners when it issued the policies. That was before my time."

"Joanna Mendler wasn't," I said, trying to regain some purchase.

"Well, maybe I did play down the fact I'd known her. But I wanted an objective Finley report. If you'd known about us, you might have bent over backward to be honest or given me something fuzzier than usual. Plus, I wouldn't be able to enjoy that look on your face right now."

That made sense—almost. "She doesn't seem to like you, Pete."

Even more graciousness. "Act like an asshole with her, and she won't like you, either. Anyway, just give me your report for my files. In case she has third thoughts. Not that I think she will. She seems to be somebody who chases one whim at a time."

"Careful now. You're slipping back into character."

"Okay, okay. By the way, did you ever find out what she was doing in that place to begin with?"

I was sorry he had asked: It reminded me of the big holes I still had in my pants. "Sure. She said she wanted to meet a hot investigator."

He laughed so hard and falsely I had to wince. I was relieved when he moved on to the usual needling about our league draft on Monday.

CHAPTER 23

The afternoon drifted toward evening. After a couple of icky sweet Tom Collinses, I stopped feeling like I had been dropped into a nest of snakes and had to be careful about making a wrong move. The food was a big help, especially a lasagna that had never seen a Stouffer's freezer. Some of my ex-teammates also got around to acknowledging that, if they hadn't had a catcher, Baker would have had a lot of wild pitches. Where I drew the line was at the dancing. Fortunately, I had Joanna and her knee as an excuse. Even Marge, who had been otherwise determined to dip into my Swiss accounts for what she kept calling "market livelies," didn't barge in once we had retreated to a corner sofa. The caption under our picture would have read: TWO FENCERS PRETENDING INTEREST IN DANCERS.

"You always look at people like a cop?"

"How does a cop look at people?"

"Like they're waiting for some telltale sign."

"Actually, it's a technique I perfected at high school dances. You'd walk into the gym, terrified out of your mind some ravishing girl would ask you to dance. So, you kept walking from one end of the place to the other, eyes up and out, pretending to be heading toward someone in particular."

She laughed. "I remember you."

I had to light a cigarette before blurting out that I couldn't say the same, that I might not have even gotten as far as the gym door if she had been on the other side.

"Answer me something? When we came in before and you looked around for the first time, you wanted to accuse me of something. What was it?" I couldn't believe I had been that obvious. "Cecile thought you were angry because she was dragging me away. But it was before she came over to us, wasn't it?"

"You're awfully alert," I said feebly.

Patsy Bowes would have accused me of condescension; Joanna Mendler merely sipped her Perrier. "I met diplomatic folk and just pompous folk at the French Academy all the time. I got very used to reading stares and tics and twitches. You'd be surprised the things that go into the simple thought—'I don't like the color of your earrings.' So, what was it you were accusing me of?"

Tommy Reynolds was back to being between us. "It never occurred to you the Reynolds kid could have been a waiter here?"

The red blossomed on the side of her neck, but nowhere else. "If you asked me right now to describe that boy behind the buffet table," she said, keeping her eyes trained on me, "I don't think I could. Maybe that makes me a snob, but it doesn't make me a conspirator in whatever you're thinking."

"I thought you were good on tics and things."

"Of important people. I just told you—I have a lot of snob in me. Excuse me."

Was it another of Sergeant Jerry Cohen's lies wrapped in a distracting truth? I couldn't guess. She bounced up so agilely and stalked away on two good knees so quickly that I was ready to believe she was all lie. And no matter how exotic it was, I didn't need it.

Chichester was rumbling his barrel to some dance that had either gone out of fashion before the musicians playing it had been born or had sneaked back into fashion while I hadn't been looking. I thought about asking him for a key to retrieve my clothes and return his, then decided I could arrange that just as easily through Piccolo or the mail. I said goodbye to anybody between the couch and the ballroom door, got a few mutterings in reply, and headed for the john in preparation for the drive back home. The john door was locked.

Since I had no intention of squirming behind the wheel in Sunday evening traffic before getting to a highway restaurant, I went looking for another bathroom at the top of the staircase where Clark Gable and Vivien Leigh had once played. The contrast upstairs from the noisy ballroom was sharper than that from leaving a stadium grandstand for an exit ramp in the middle of a game. This particular ramp was completely carpeted and lighted along the way by those carriage lights the architect had had second, fourth, and twelfth thoughts about. Every 15 feet along the corridor, there was an enormous painting—mostly Revolutionary and Civil war scenes. I figured it was 50-50 the Bakers had a long military tradition or the last interior decorator had a contact in some upscale junk shop.

The first door I opened was for a linen closet with enough bedding for a Hilton. The next one was for a bedroom that didn't seem to have a bathroom attached. The third one was for a sitting room where, to judge from the opened books on a coffee table and tea set on a dolly, the Bakers spent their more modest leisure hours. Then I walked into a miniature screening room. It was miniature because there was a giant TV screen instead of the pulldown affair I've always had my eye on for my first mansion and because the shelves were filled with cassettes instead of old film reels. Another switch: There were couches, not slip-slide chairs, arrayed in three rows before the TV screen.

I told my bladder to wait a minute.

The first shelf to the left of the door was for every musical comedy ever made by MGM. Then came the shelves for Astaire, Gable, Tracy, Stewart, Bogart, and Cooper. By the time I got to the Stanwyck collection, my ferret started getting impatient. He knew what we were looking for.

The porn turned out to take up half the right wall. First came the outside productions, with titles like *Bush Pilots* and *Hole in Two*. Then bullseye: at least a hundred personally labeled tapes along two rows in the far right-hand corner. It took me a second to see they were arranged alphabetically—BARBARA, BARBARA II, CHARLIE, DEIDRE, FRANK. I skipped to the second part of the alphabet, knowing with a sweat what I was going to find. The only choice I ended up having was whether to pull out TOM or TOMMY first. I settled on TOMMY.

"What does your taste run to?"

Cecile Baker was standing in the doorway, what weight she had resting fully on the doorknob. She was thin to the point of scrawniness, but her swept-back brown hair accentuated an oddly big head. "Mickey Rooney. Judy Garland."

"Really? What's your favorite?"

"*The Wizard of Oz.*"

Her eyes dropped to the cassette in my hand, but her squint said she could barely make out the box, let alone the title. "Mickey Rooney wasn't in that."

"Great character actor. He played the magic broom. Who's in this one? I never heard of it."

She leaned off the door and took two quick strides inside. She might not have been able to read the title of the cassette while it was in my hand, but she saw the hole in the shelf between TOM and URSULA. "As I'm sure an intelligent man like yourself has worked out," she said airily, "that's a private tape. I think you should leave it. Willy doesn't mind friends borrowing other things, but the private things are . . ."

"Private?"

"Exactly. But if it's Judy Garland you're looking for, I think we have a tape of one of her television shows not on the market yet. Where would we have put that . . .?"

I had a few seconds of leeway to pretend to put TOMMY back on the shelf while sticking it under my shirt. But I had always been a lousy shoplifter, and Tony Camerino's shirt didn't make me a better one. For a second I was sorry Chichester *hadn't* left me Bozo the clown's outfit. I settled on the next best solution: sticking the cassette back where it belonged so I would know exactly where to find it when I made a second pass without Cecile around.

"Never mind, Cecile. I always liked her better as an actress than a singer. Right now, I could use a bathroom."

"Oh," she said, looking genuinely disappointed in my taste. "Right across the hall there."

"Thanks."

I pissed out my ferret. I didn't need his help anymore. Throwing some water on my face made me see The Professional Finley in the bathroom mirror. I had marked the field as clearly as possible, and now just had to take it a step at a time:

Step 1: sneak back into the screening room and get the tape of Tommy Reynolds.

Step 2: confirm the tape showed Tommy screwing with Cecile, Willy Baker, both, or others.

Step 3: give the tape to Ellen Miles.

Step 4: pick up *Newsday* and read about the Bakers being led in for questioning for organizing sex parties with minors that ended, once anyway, in homicide.

Step 5: pick up *Newsday* and read about a confession from one of the Bakers, Scarecrow, or somebody else that, yes, indeed, things had gotten out of hand during a tryst in the woods and the only solution at hand had been a big rock.

And Step 6?

Maybe stay away from Mary Reynolds and hope that, one day, she would be able to forget about me along with everybody and everything else connected to her brother's murder.

CHAPTER 24

I went back downstairs trying to look like somebody who hadn't been in that much of a hurry to leave, after all. Chichester was still boogying or frugging or flopping, which eliminated the possibility of his abruptly calling it a day and forcing me to leave with him to reclaim my clothes. He wasn't going to have a stroke; he was going to drown in all the sweat he was drenching the floor with around him.

I was making my way over to one of the bar tables for something cold and nonalcoholic when Baker jumped up on the bandstand to wave the musicians quiet. The clamor stopped mid-note, making for a general moaning from the dancers and leaving Chichester, in particular, to look like he was about to topple off the edge of a cliff.

"Okay, everybody," Baker announced, "time to get down to the serious fun. Skins and Shirts! I need four hitters!"

The uproar from the floor immediately consigned the dancing to the remote past. The musicians caught on: As one, they began packing up their instruments.

"Fred, I'll take you," Baker said, acknowledging the publishing guy's hand. "What about you, Bob?"

Chichester was actually doing waist bends to retrieve his air. Despite that, he waved okay. What he was waving to exactly I wasn't sure, outside of the fact that "Skins and Shirts" were how we had once played basketball as gangly teenagers in the schoolyard. I couldn't believe even Chichester would defy his heart muscles that much.

Baker was suddenly peering over the crowd at me. "I saw your glove, Finley," he shouted merrily, "but that's not going to be any help here. What about you, Robin?"

Whatever it was, I was being left out of it, and that was just fine with the heads that had turned around to me with Baker's acknowledgment: They couldn't forget about me quickly enough to go back to the bandstand with cries for attention.

"Short-lived glory," Joanna, next to me, muttered.

I told myself there would be time to be pissed about that later. More important, the room seemed on the verge of being emptied out for some new exercise and that promised the opportunity to go back upstairs for the tape. My last worry on that score vanished at the sight of Cecile entering the room and giggling with Marge over something.

"How about dropping me back to my car? I think I've had enough jock talk for the day."

"I want to hang on for a couple of minutes."

"For this?"

"What exactly is this?"

A cheer went up from the room as Baker selected somebody else. "I won't spoil your curiosity," she said, wandering off again.

I was about to go after her, to ask for five minutes max, when the rush started toward the French doors behind the bandstand. All I had glimpsed out there was endless lawn; not a single basketball hoop. But I didn't care about that. I turned around to drag out my loitering with a request for another ginger ale. But the bartender was gone. As was every other waiter in the room.

I waited until Cecile moved outside with everybody else, told myself it was a positive sign she didn't throw me any pregnant looks, then headed back upstairs.

And was too late.

Every single one of the privately marked cassettes was gone.

I dithered. It seemed more manly than getting down on the floor and sobbing. I opened a few cabinets but found nothing inside except blank tapes, VCR accessories, and, for some reason, an old pamphlet describing the anti-abortion intentions of the Operation Salvation zealots. It was heartening to see the Bakers were readers as much as cinephiles.

There was a bellowing from the back lawn outside the window, but I didn't care if Chichester had already taken his dive for the EMS. Instead, I pictured Cecile explaining to Miles and Levine how she hadn't known she was ditching evidence in a homicide case. The image lasted for all of five seconds. Thanks to my stupidity, Cecile Baker wouldn't have to be explaining anything to Miles and Levine.

I went back downstairs. I had no further excuse for not driving Joanna back to her car. If I played my cards right, I thought, she might even tell me another lie.

Darkness had fallen enough for a string of field lights to be turned on at the far end of the lawn. Every last soul from the party was gathered around my third mirage on the day—a batting cage straight from Coney Island. Baker even had a protective pitching screen as he fired toward the plate. The batter was one of the waiters or musicians—a Bolero, in any case. Other Boleros, the publishing guy Fred, and Marge were scattered around the lawn retrieving the batted balls.

I stopped midway over. Was it possible I had been exaggerating everything? That all I had seen on the day were the Chichesters and the Bakers with their brains down? Why couldn't the TOMMY tape have been the batting cage record of a Tommy Smith or Tommy Jones?

I trudged on toward the batting cage not sure what I wanted to believe, what I could believe, and what the difference was between the two. It was the waiter named Kevin in the batter's box, and he had eyes only for destroying whatever Baker threw up at him. I spotted Joanna on the far side of the cage, and signaled I was ready to go. She nodded behind a final few words to Cecile, and I couldn't help thinking she was getting a report from the lady of the house on her friend's wanderings in the screening room.

Kevin hit one last shot well over Fred's head, drawing a general intake of breath from everyone except Cecile, who kept talking, and Joanna, who kept listening. "Okay, Kev," Baker yelled in. "Practice is over. Let's start. You have your team?"

"Yes, sir. Five, right?"

Baker nodded as Kevin pointed to the petite Gloria, a buxom blonde who had been playing the guitar, and two other Boleros. He then turned back to those who had been running after the practice shots. "Only the Shirts stay out there! Everybody else off until the next game!"

The Boleros, Marge, and a couple of others drifted off toward the sidelines. Kevin was pulled to one side by Gloria and the blonde, who seemed to be complaining about something. He listened for a second, shrugged, then looked out at Baker. "Mr. Baker, why can't we be the Shirts and you the Skins?"

There was a sarcastic tittering behind me. I turned to see who it was but saw only two of the waiters arriving in double time with more drinks.

"Because the Shirts are always the home team," Baker shouted back. "You own this place, you're the home team. I own it, so we are. Come on now. Get into uniform so we can start."

Scarecrow waved away the waiter impatiently; he had eyes only for Kevin and the two girls. Others removed their drinks from the tray mechanically. Gloria listened to some urgent muttering from Kevin, then from one of the other boys on the team. Her eyes hugged the ground as she began unbuttoning her blouse.

"Okay, let's have Gina first!" Baker yelled in. "You'll be the cleanup hitter, Kevin!"

Kevin's last stand as he unbuttoned his own shirt was a glazed-eye sneer at Baker. "Gloria! Her name is Gloria!"

"Can we go now?"

Joanna was searching my face for more than I dared show her. I could believe she was more snob than liar. I *had* to believe it.

We were just in the way of the gleeful spectators as we made our way back toward the French doors. We were blocking their view of Gloria's tits jiggling as she swung at Baker's first delivery.

CHAPTER 25

It was a 15-minute run over to the main square to pick up her car; it felt like 15 hours. I still didn't have any harder evidence for Miles, of course; just a harder repugnance. And even that left out a lot. It was still the 21st century. Not even wildly hormonal teenagers were indentured servants. They didn't have to be. So why had they become so vulnerable to the blandishments of the Baker crowd?

The cop Finley kicked in: It was never sex; it was always power. But the cop Finley had no idea about what power.

"I need your help on something," I blurted.

She had been waiting for me to make the first sound, and sighed with relief. "What?"

"The names of those people. All of them."

I wasn't there for whatever she was asking with her suspicions; the main street traffic took care of that. "I don't know them all."

"The ones you know will be a good start."

She turned back to the windshield. "All right."

I don't know what I would have said if she had told me to go to hell, but I was surprised by her quick agreement—surprised and already thinking about how to move on to the second front of Richie Clary. As the Professor might have said, it was going to have to be a pincer attack: Dig into the raincoat brigade from Xanadu at one end and press the Clary kid at the other. Somewhere in between was Tommy Reynolds's body.

"You'll need your clothes," she said, when we arrived back at the square. The red lights from Danny's saloon had fallen over her forehead like a colorful but blank X-ray. I could make anything at all of what I saw.

"Not really."

She shrugged and opened the door. "Whatever."

She got out, slammed the door without looking back, and walked over to her car searching for her keys in her bag. I knew I was going to follow her back to Chichester's place, but with a reason—an ennobling reason.

The reason occurred to me as she was pulling out of her space: I *needed* more than I had.

After the Baker house, even Chichester's presidential retreat felt like something built for human beings. As I retrieved my torn pants and shirt and put them back on, I had no idea how that had happened. By any odds, whatever the Bakers were up to, Chichester was right in the middle of it with them.

When I returned to the main room, she was sitting on one of the divans, bobbing her good leg up and down off the bum one and blowing smoke like a dragon. "Some place I can put these?" I asked, showing her my bundle of Tony Camerino's shirt and jeans.

"I told you: I'm not the housekeeper around here."

I had assumed there was another bathroom in the back earlier, so I went back to confirm it also had a hamper. It did.

"What is it exactly you think you found tonight?" she asked as soon as I came out again. "That I play their games?"

"To be honest, I've been thinking of you as only one of the extras."

That was worth another bob of her knee. "Wonderful."

"You socialize with them, Joanna, and they seem to like socializing with you."

"I socialize with you too, but I don't have a hole in my pants."

The choice seemed to be more repartee or leaving; I headed for the door. "I'd appreciate that list. It could be a big help."

"You don't know there's any connection!"

She was up on her feet and glaring; it wasn't repartee I had been walking away from, but fury. "I do. And you do."

"Then I'll leave with you." She detested my dithering look. "I'm a widow, Finley, not a black widow. Or maybe you just walk around needing to believe all survivors are murderers."

Whatever I had built up inside crumbled. I couldn't get over to her fast enough. But she stood her ground. Brazen. Defiant. Daring me to slap her—and knowing I had already used up that energy just getting to her. "Give me a second," she said, making it sound like a sentence. "I have to put my things in a bag."

"You have a . . ."

"That's Robert's car. You'll have to give me a lift."

She had so many definitive announcements I was starting to feel like the villager listening to the daily proclamation from the king's messenger. I grabbed her before she could start off for the bedroom. She had been holding on to me on the softball field and again on our way to The Rook, but it felt like the first time I had touched her. "I'm not up for it, Joanna. One maze I'll get myself out of eventually. Two? I'm past my prime."

The royals had mercy. "I don't know anything about this murdered boy," she said, measuring every syllable. "And I don't know anything about the kids we just left. But if you're so sure there's a connection with someone from today, I know where I would start looking. And it wouldn't be with Robert or Willy."

We were back to the collision at home plate. "That's crazy."

"You work for him, I don't."

The ploys were endless. The subterfuges crawled within one another and out again. And Mr. and Mrs. Black and Mama Nerone had nothing to do with them. "You're carrying your resentment pretty far, aren't you?"

I took my hand off her wrist, but she grabbed mine. "I hate Pete Piccolo, Finley," she said, seeming to want it on the record of my pulse. "You know how much I hate him? I have fantasies all the time of hurting him. Worse than you hurt him today. Much, much worse."

I was competing, and competing as an underdog: I knew it right away. Whatever torment Piccolo had tapped in her guilts about Harold Mendler had been a gusher. But it didn't matter, not after her tongue was waiting there for mine and her hip bone managed to penetrate even my corduroys.

CHAPTER 26

We were two entire pickup teams clutching at one another. Beyond Harold Mendler, I didn't want to think about who was on her side. And I already had enough trouble trying not to think about Jennifer, what had promised to be with Ellen Miles, and what might have been with whomever if I had been open to more than street signs and red lights since the accident. If I succeeded in dismissing all the choose-up distractions, maybe it was because I found at least one piece of truth in everything when I slipped off her pants and saw the bandage around her knee. "Take it off," she whispered. The knee was discolored. She smiled as proudly as I suddenly felt.

I nodded off at one point, then was aware of opening my eyes as she slipped off the bed. The second time was more complete: I popped up totally awake, panicked she wasn't with me, then relaxed to see her at the window. She had her bare legs and feet up on the sill, a green cardigan thrown over her shoulders. She was blowing smoke at the morning light breaking over the ocean.

I started to ask if Chichester had come back, then remembered I didn't care.

"Tell me who you are, Finley."

I knew where I was going right away, but I drew it out a little, just so I could reassure myself I wasn't completely defined by Jennifer and Susan. It worked for a minute or so, until she pulled the foot of her good leg into her and examined her instep for something more interesting.

"It was the usual Christmas dinner. My wife, daughter, and father-in-law. Jennifer and I wanted to go to a restaurant, but the Professor insisted he was going to cook. It was his big test. He hadn't cooked anything since his wife had died the year before, and he wasn't going to postpone his 'coming out,' as he called it, for any restaurant. He laid it on thick. Turkey, dressing, everything. He wouldn't let Jennifer or me do anything but open the wine. I did a lot of opening. Joe Carroll's a great cook, but even on normal days it takes him forever. That Christmas wasn't normal. Jennifer kept throwing me eye signals not to say anything, even as a joke. I left it up to Susan. She complained enough for all of us."

"Is that what you called her—Jennifer?"

"Joe always called her that. Never Jenny or anything like that. I guess I got into the habit. The only one who didn't was this neighbor of ours who had one cutesy name after another. If it wasn't Jenny or Jen, it was J or J-Fer. Jennifer hated it."

"Why didn't she tell your neighbor to stop?"

Because she wasn't Joanna Mendler, was the real answer. "When she could avoid conflict, she did."

She released her foot with a nod as if she hadn't expected any other answer.

"Anyway, by the time the food got to the table, I was pretty sloshed. The dinner was great, but it didn't help much. Then, after dinner, the Professor unveiled his special-special cognac to celebrate this coming out of his. The time just flew. Susan kept going back and forth to play with the kids next door. Jennifer started in on the dishes and seemed to want to work her way up to cleaning the attic. Joe kept talking. I kept drinking. The last thing I remember was throwing up in the bathroom and flopping into the Professor's bed."

She lighted another cigarette without looking at me. I glued my eyes to her light brown pubic hair, to the soft pull of her stomach muscles as she moved around in the chair.

"Jennifer insisted on driving home. Said she wanted Susan to sleep in her own bed. The old man says they had a fight, but I don't think so. He and Jennifer never had fights. They might exchange a barb or two, but then they'd get out of one another's way. Anyway, the roads were icy. They were supposed to have died right away."

She waited for something else from the Atlantic outside.

"She was sober. They ruled that out right away."

She was still waiting for something.

"The Professor blames himself for not waking me up and making me drive them home."

That was what she had been waiting for. "So you could have been killed, too?"

"I guess that's in there somewhere. In both of us. If the bastard had only cooked faster and talked less . . . Like that."

"You certainly watch your drinking now."

"Sometimes I think that's an affectation," I heard myself saying. "If you're a drunk, you can salvage something for the wee hours by not being a drunk anymore. When you just got potted one Christmas, you have to hang your stocking out a helluva long time in advance even to delude yourself things will get better."

"I thought you were describing an accident."

"I don't believe in them, Joanna."

"The residue of design?"

"Something like that. We were getting pretty rocky for a year or so before. Not that we . . ."

"Exactly. Not that you were. All that's irrelevant."

She planted the foot of her bad knee up on the window and winced at the pull. "It's almost there," she said, approvingly.

"Tell me something? Who did you used to be?"

She smiled into her cigarette. "Very stylish. Very ladylike. And also very passive. I missed the age of white gloves, but college and the academy were pretty close. Then one night there was a reception at the French Embassy to the UN. Harold was there because he did some business with one of the French banks. He said he liked the style and the lady, but I was going to be nothing more than a social hostess with different titles if I didn't learn to say what I had on my mind and act on it. He was terribly seductive when he said that. Maybe it was then and there, maybe it was 10 seconds later, but I fell in love with him." She dropped her leg. "I won't go through a thing like that again, Finley."

"So sure?"

She snapped to so quickly I might have been a cigarette spark falling on her belly. "You're not listening. I'm *none* of the people I used to be."

She dashed out the cigarette and stood up. The only difference from the day at the pool was that she wasn't wearing a bathing suit.

And that I didn't have my tape recorder. "Why *were* you in the Cameo?"

She threw off the sweater and climbed back into the bed. "Maybe I was getting away from somebody."

"Who?"

"That's none of your business."

"How much of a coincidence was the Cameo? Piccolo says some of the same people at the party are the ones behind the Cameo and that video store I was talking about."

She burrowed under the covers and gave off a shiver. "That's no coincidence at all," she said casually. "Those people at the party, their relatives and friends, are behind everything on Long Island. If I hadn't spent a long time with his papers, I wouldn't be able to say flat out that Harold wasn't behind the movie house and your video store."

"Would you still have filed your claim?"

The dawning light had nothing on her dismay. "Why not? I was the one who hurt my knee, not the investors. But I really don't want to talk about that anymore. It's over."

I hadn't noticed before how chilly the room was. But it didn't matter after a couple of seconds.

CHAPTER 27

As soon as I got home and straightened myself out a little, I called Ellen Miles and asked her to meet me in the coffee shop near her office where we had once eaten more than a healthy share of pastramis on rye. She was less than enthusiastic. When I made some unsubtle allusions to what she had told me at the mall, she questioned my intelligence altogether, but agreed to come.

The coffee shop owner Myron made it awkward going for a couple of minutes with reminiscences of old sandwiches, but backed away when we ordered only coffees. I opened the bidding with the list of names Joanna had given me before I had dropped her home. I then went into my Sunday adventures with the Baker crowd. Ellen listened with a studied indifference. I might not have expected a grandstand ovation, but I had counted on at least a raised eyebrow or two.

"I'm still waiting," she said after I had finished.

"I'm giving you what I have."

"Which is nothing."

"Think I didn't want to come here with that tape? Sorry, I fucked up. But it's still in that house somewhere."

"Out in Suffolk County, you mean? The Suffolk County that doesn't happen to be part of Nassau County? Where they breed them so stupid they even hang on to incriminating evidence instead of burning it? Of course, we're getting ahead of ourselves there, aren't we? This zillionaire just *might* own a tape starring our victim. The victim just *might* be seen in the act with the zillionaire, his wife, or one of their friends. Or might this Tommy just be some nephew filmed on a yacht in the Sound or waving to us from the Grand Canyon?"

I had anticipated some barrage of the kind; in her place, I would have said the same things. But she had put a little more passion into it than I had foreseen, and she still hadn't looked too closely at the list of names next to her cup. "I've never come to you with bullshit, Ellen. You want to play games to prove you're a good soldier, go ahead. But don't kid yourself you're doing it for professional reasons."

She relented enough to gaze out the window. "We're developing other leads," she announced. "There's this neighbor."

"Old man Gregg? You got to be kidding!"

"Fire Department retired him a few years early because he couldn't keep his hands off the neighborhood kids who hung around the firehouse."

I didn't know what that was about, and it dismayed me, but I also remembered Gregg's tears in Tommy's room. They hadn't been remorse tears; they had been sorrow tears: I would have bet anything on it. "That's crap."

"Why? Because he goes to church every Sunday?"

I dove for my cup. Her question came out of some swamp that had little to do with police cynicism. I might have almost believed she and hubby Mr. Ambitious didn't like Gregg's slipshod commitments to the sterner demands of Mother Church and weren't beyond showing him the error of his ways publicly. "Who's running the case for the DA?" I asked, not sounding casual even to myself.

"Not my husband, if that's what you mean."

"Good. I wouldn't want him getting his conscience in knots about investigating people he might know from a picket line or a group rosary."

"What's that supposed to mean?"

"I'm not sure. But while I was nosing around the Baker place, I came across some of the zealot literature your man seems to believe in. What's it called—Operation . . .?"

She seemed to count to three before deciding to stay where she was. "Somebody who believes in nothing shouldn't be so disapproving of people who believe in something."

"But I do believe in things, Ellen. I believe in old boy networks. I believe in standup guys. I believe there are some people out there who can blend their ambition and self-righteousness together into a fine paste. And I believe those same people don't want to embarrass other people even more self-righteous than they are if it helps their ambition."

"You've got a more immediate problem," she said imperturbably. "I hear you talked to Gregg under the pretense of being a policeman."

"That's weak, hon."

"But it's true, isn't it?"

"He assumed. I didn't contradict him. Can we get back to the point now?"

"Gregg has a prior. That's the point."

"Solid. Definitely something to pursue. Jesus would approve."

"You're really screwed up, Paul. You know that?"

"No argument. I didn't even know how much until yesterday. Here I am watching these platinum card thrill-seekers—not great thrills, you understand, the cheap kind Tommy Reynolds had in his skin magazines—here I am watching them slavering to get a look at a teenager's tits or maybe her boyfriend's dick, and I wanted to lead the next crusade against them. Just because it made *me* feel small being in their company. Out, out, cursed spot, that kind of thing, you know? But the funny thing is, here I've just set out some of the same sordid details for you, somebody with a real sharp vision of what's morally okay and what isn't, and you haven't blinked once."

"I've been on this job long enough not to be surprised by anything."

"One possibility. Or maybe you heard these sordid details before and I'm not bringing anything new to the table. And then let's admit a third possibility—you've already found the perfect pigeon for solving a homicide, easing department pressures on you, and relaxing some of that existential anguish at home."

"You really believe I'd let my private beliefs . . .?"

"What I know, Ellen, is that if I gave you a list like that a couple of years ago, you would've sat there nodding me to death and kept sneaking glances at those names to see how many might be on your Christmas card list. But this morning you haven't been the least bit curious. That's fabulous for office politics and religious zealotry, but not too hot for your average detective." I had to get away from her—and from whoever was sitting on her shoulder. "Do me a favor and get a little curious again, okay? If for no other reason than to satisfy yourself, you're not railroading Gregg. Believe me, Jesus wouldn't approve of that."

Once back on the street I didn't know if I had exaggerated the intramural interests of Mr. and Mrs. Miles or not. What I was sure about was that something had happened since the mall fire that wouldn't permit her to spill the latest gossip even with the back of her head.

And then came a lousy thought: The one good result of Jennifer's accident was that I hadn't gotten in more deeply with the present Mrs. Miles.

I didn't mind the lousy thought.

CHAPTER 28

I probably should have gone directly from the coffee shop to see Mary Reynolds, but Ellen's announcement about Gregg gave me a reason for putting that off. There were sure to be reporters, cops, and a legion of thrill seekers swarming over both houses, and that didn't seem like the right setting for Mary to explode at me for not helping to save her brother or for Gregg to explode at me for contributing to his problems. Besides, if I was ever going to have maneuvering room for getting more out of Richie Clary, it was while Miles and Levine were preoccupied with Gregg.

I phoned the kid's school to make sure April 2 wasn't a special holiday for the county supervisor or LIRR conductor who had lent his name to the place. Fifteen minutes before the woman on the phone had said it was let out time, I took up surveillance across the street from the school's main entrance. When I got tired of looking at the slate gray building and the two security guards chewing the fat near the door, I made a stab at writing down my priorities for our draft meeting that evening. My brain wasn't into it. I listed the usual 15 or 20 suspects I didn't need to write down to remember, then admitted I was going to be winging it anyway. But even that half-exercise was good for two things. In looking at all the obvious all-star names, I realized Joanna had left the obvious name of Pete Piccolo off her list. And that in turn reminded me that Piccolo had been nowhere to be seen during the Batting Cage Follies. Was either item significant? I hoped not, if only because Swifty Finley might have been accused still once again of having been asleep at the switch.

When the kids started seeping out, they came not just from the main entrance, but from two auxiliary doors I hadn't noticed. It was the usual scene of the clown running out and praising Allah from his knees for liberating him from chemistry lab, the mad scientist whacking the back of his leg with a schoolbag that seemed to be carrying a ton of iron, the Nicotine Nicks with cigarettes going before they were even through the door. When was it I had been ready to believe every teenager on the Island was hustling or being hustled by the likes of Willy Baker? Now I was back to the Donna Reed Show.

Richie Clary came out flanked by a pair of redheads who looked like brother-sister twins. He seemed to be as moody toward them as he had been toward me and Mary Reynolds. The three of them crossed over to the other side of the street, where the girl took out keys for an old red Pontiac. Why I had expected to get Clary alone before he got home, I didn't know. I had little choice but to follow the Pontiac.

The girl had apparently taken her driving lessons from Mr. Rogers. She was so cautious she even stopped at a green light for a woman who had barely stepped off the sidewalk to wave her across. I was beginning to think we were heading for the home of the twins for a glass of milk and some nice strawberry cupcakes.

We weren't. Crawling miles later, we were entering Uniondale, where the Pontiac pulled up before a video rental store. The drab sign said Star Video. I hadn't thought of the mall place as part of a chain, but that was obviously what it was. Clary and the boy twin got out of the car and went inside.

My first thought was that Star Video had found jobs in its other outlets for the kids who had been burned out of a salary at the mall. That held up for about two seconds—until the twin started casing the shelves while Clary meandered directly over to a bulletin board, found something he was looking for and took it down. All I could make out was that it was an index card and that he was squashing it into his pocket as he and the twin wandered right out again.

After Uniondale came Roosevelt, and the same routine in a place called Martha's Video. I decided not to keep playing the caboose, and took off just as Clary and his friend were returning to the Pontiac. When I got to Freeport, I drove around for a few minutes hoping to get lucky with another Star Video franchise. I didn't get lucky. There was one store that said only Video on a sign, another called Jack's, and a third by the name of Hollywood Video. The redhead might have been driving like a snail, but I still had time for only one of them. I stuck to the brand name—Hollywood Video.

It was the right choice. An index card on the store's bulletin board said: WAITERS, WAITRESSES, MUSICIANS NEEDED FOR HOUSE SOCIALS. MUST BE WILLING TO WORK WEEKENDS, LONG HOURS. ATHLETIC SKILLS A PLUS.

I copied down the phone number on the card just as the Pontiac drove up outside. I was still thinking too slowly. Whatever her other reasons for stonewalling, I had also struck out with Miles because I hadn't had the tape to show her. Even if she wanted to claim I had been the one to type it up, I needed the card itself for her.

"Hey, brother! Anything you put up there or take down has to be cleared with the management!"

In another life, the bulky woman in the black dress behind the counter had been Anna Magnani. Her look said she hadn't spent a single day of her 50 years without having to suffer the torments of characters screwing up her bulletin board. "It's an old notice. We don't need waiters anymore."

"Let me see what you got there."

The door opened before I could stick the card out of sight. Richie Clary started when he saw me. He didn't seem to feel the pain that must have hit his heels or calves when the boy twin walked right up his legs. I had seen his expression before, but couldn't remember from where.

He turned and walked back out to the Pontiac. The twin studied me for a second, thought of nothing pertinent, then hurried out after Clary.

"They supposed to be home doing homework for you or something?" Magnani asked. "What did you catch them at?"

At Finley blowing a chance to talk to Richie Clary, I thought. "I just want it for my files," I told her as she snatched the card from me for a closer look. "Won't have to type it up the next time I need it."

"You're not the one who posted this."

"That was my partner. He puts them up, I take them down. That's why we're partners."

"Wrong. *I* put them up and *I* take them down."

"Right. I forgot."

She couldn't smell a felony and she had no time for misdemeanors. "Your partner's quite the gay blade," she said, handing me back the card. "He always wear a bra under his blouse?"

Cecile Baker. "Must have been his wife."

"Let's hope so."

"Have a nice day."

"Can't get any nicer than it's been so far."

I went to the pay phone on the corner and punched out the number on the index card. A formal voice belonging to a middle-aged man replied with the news that I had reached the "Baker residence." When I asked who he was, he sounded miffed to have to identify himself as "Arthur the houseman." I hadn't seen a trace of Arthur on Sunday.

I hung up and stood for a moment to contemplate my next move. I had now firmly established it was Baker who had posted the ads in the video stores. In other words, I had just firmly established that Abraham Lincoln had been the 16th President of the United States.

CHAPTER 29

We held our fantasy league draft in Al Chiozza's basement. He was the last cop remaining from my original pigeons at the station house. Chiozza had been in Traffic for most of my cop years, but had broken his hip in a fall and been assigned every inside job conceivable—switchboard, booking desk, community relations, warrant processing. As far as he had been concerned, one was indistinguishable from the other in its potential for driving him nuts and only the fact that he had been a year away from his pension had stifled his relentless requests for anything at all outside. We got along because I had sneaked him into my car several times when I had been out on something. In return, he had always relayed weather reports from his old contacts on the winds blowing around the chief's office.

Another reason I liked Chiozza: Being almost as old as the Professor, he sensed his leverage—with me as an appreciative audience—for being able to tell Joe Carroll when to go to hell. Despite the Professor's grumblings over this or that Chiozza dig, I had always had the feeling that if they had lived closer to one another, they would have spent more than one afternoon together comparing skepticisms about the human race.

I could tell as soon as we walked in the side door to the kitchen that Chiozza had a weather report for me. More than usual, he didn't listen to his wife's obligatory cracks about overaged kids stinking up her basement with smoke; totally uncharacteristic, he tried to be charming about telling the Professor to go down to the basement to claim the best seat. The Professor considered it sufficient to see through so much politeness and clomped on downstairs.

"You got trouble," Chiozza announced as soon as we were alone.

"Miles and Levine?"

"That you should expect by now," he said, getting a couple of beers from the refrigerator and tossing me one. "Levine still thinks you fucked up his bris. I'm talking upstairs. There's been at least one look at your license."

"Why, Al?"

He slumped against the sink and threw down almost half his can. "The Reynolds kid. What else?"

"Yeah, but what in particular about the Reynolds kid?"

He wiped the back of his hand across his mouth with what was probably his umpteenth consideration of what he was about to say. "I think you ought to get out to the movies more, kid. Leave home videos to others."

"Riddles. I've already got too many of them, man."

He thought that was reasonable, but still wasn't about to dump himself out with the bathwater. He patted his big belly to remind himself he still expected to eat every once in a while. "I always preferred fairy tales to riddles," he said finally. "One of my favorites, for instance, is about these bored rich people who are sitting around one day and decide they're not doing enough for society. All that awful crime and terrorism out there. All these welfare cheats. Where's yesterday's morality? When're people going to get back to understanding what's right and what's wrong? Not that they consider themselves saints, mind you. They know they've winked an eye here and there when it's been to their benefit. But now they're no longer young hotshots climbing the corporate ladder. How many more oil stocks can they possibly need? They're getting on in years, getting nearer and nearer the day when their specialist will tell them their lights are going out. And then what are they going to have to show the Great Accountant in the sky?"

"So they decide to invest in the inner city and build it up so everybody gets a decent life?"

Chiozza gave me his little hyena laugh. "You can tell me your fairy tale after I finish mine. No, what they do is look around for an issue—some one thing they think they can all get behind to enrich their souls. And they find that issue, capital **I**. One that's very popular with the kind of cassocks who can endorse them with the Great Accountant. A very safe issue that won't cost them with the politicos they manipulate and depend on because who's going to tell the money man he can't act in good conscience on behalf of his immortal soul?"

"The pro-lifers."

Chiozza ignored me; as I would have ignored me. "Being successful businessmen in a thousand different things, though, creates a small problem. They need a center, some common source of funding for their charitable work. They're not usually into retail, but there is one kind of business a lot of them have flirted with at one time or another, if only to cover their taxes. So, they decide this will be the funding source, and every penny they make from that business will go into their issue, capital **I**. Some cassocks are so grateful for this initiative they have every parish house on the Island equipped with a VCR. Just to see *Going My Way*, you understand."

"Sounds like a happy ending."

"It should have been," he said behind a satisfying belch. "But then this Bigfoot arrives and starts poking around in the retail business everybody wants to succeed. That doesn't sit well with anybody, especially when Bigfoot seems determined to connect this worthy moral endeavor to a very ugly killing. As Lindbergh once said, that just ain't gonna fly."

"Save me another trip to the record office, Al. Who owns Star Video?"

He hadn't noticed before that I spoke only Greek. "Star what? Drink your beer, Finley. It's just getting hot in your hand there."

The side door closed with a bang, and Gil Stedina stuck his nose in. "Where's the action? Where's the action?"

Chiozza didn't lose the chance to lead Stedina downstairs to the basement to get away from me.

CHAPTER 30

Counting the Professor and me, there were eight of us. In addition to Chiozza and Stedina, there were two cousins of Chiozza's, a Gramercy man named Kimberly, and Piccolo. Normally, the chief sideshow at the drafts was one of Chiozza's cousins—a bullet-headed guy named Forte who was a poster for manic depression. Forte's idea of conversation was a reluctant hello when he arrived, a money figure during the bidding, and a relieved goodbye when he left. Otherwise, he sat in what was usually the most uncomfortable, worst lighted spot available, gloomily poring over his prepared lists of players and ignoring the banter around him. According to Chiozza, Forte's problem was that he had worked in a library as a maintenance man too long and had taken too much to heart the need for silence. It was a glib diagnosis, but about as interested as Chiozza had ever professed to be about his cousin. Or as he put it to me and the Professor once, "Just don't hand him a chainsaw and we won't have to think about him."

But this time Forte had serious competition in the depression stakes. From the second he entered the basement and moved to the patio chair furthest away from the table where Chiozza and Kimberly were recording everything, Piccolo looked like he was in pain. I didn't mind the thought he was still aching from our collision, but it didn't take me long to see his problem was more mental than physical. I had never known him to be so distracted—not even when he had been breaking up with his wife. The Professor caught on when Barry Bonds was on the table: Piccolo started with a bid of three dollars, then ended up spending more than half his roll to get what he wanted. Over the last hour he was hard put to bid more than a dollar or two for any player, leaving him with Bonds and players as likely to be on the bench as on the playing field. The Professor continued to sneak looks at me to ask what was going on. The strange thing was, I felt I should have known.

The one most delighted by Piccolo's erratic tactics was Kimberly, who worked in Gramercy's personnel department. He couldn't wait to register every transaction so he could remind Piccolo how much less money he had for subsequent transactions. During a bathroom break, we did a little Laurel and Hardy trying to pass one another in Chiozza's narrow hallway, and Kimberly's idea of small talk was to ask me whether he or I would end up with Piccolo's money.

"It's a long season," I told him, sounding like Father Time.

"Not that long. The signs are clear; the signs are clear."

I was glad to get back down into the basement. Even his mirth seemed like some guilty secret. Did Gramercy grow them *all* like that?

The Professor found out more than I did. Driving home, he broke off his self-satisfaction with his roster long enough to ruminate about Gramercy's employment picture. "According to Kimberly, Piccolo can't keep his fly shut. He was bitching to me about all the receptionists and secretaries he must keep processing. Seems they have to have two qualifications where your friend is concerned—long legs and a pedigree."

"Pedigree?"

"Only from the best families. But then he hires them and either they can't get enough of him or get more than enough."

"What do you mean—can't get enough of him?"

"I'm just repeating what Kimberly said."

"Repeat it."

He shrugged. "The conquest mentality, I suppose. Fuck 'em once and that makes them no longer interesting."

"Why do I think that's bullshit? Why don't I see old-love-em-and-leave-em Pete when I look at Piccolo? Sounds like Kimberly has his own hard-on for something."

"You don't have to get so testy about it. Maybe it's the oppo-site—the women get one look at his action and quit. One way or another, Kimberly says he has to pay for a lot of want ads."

I had noticed the turnover in receptionists, too, of course. But the Professor had also been right about my testiness. There was something about Piccolo as Romeo that bothered me as much as Willy Baker slobbering over Gloria in the batting cage. Condescension and anger came together in its usual curdle of contempt, and I didn't mind it laying there.

CHAPTER 31

The phone was ringing in the basement when we walked in. As I went downstairs, I was sure it was Joanna, and didn't know whether her calling first was her weakness or mine. I could have saved myself the philosophical question because it turned out to be a very tense Chichester.

"You're upsetting a lot of people," he said, sounding midway between the poolside attorney and my teammate.

"Yeah, that seems to be the consensus."

Silence. Then: "We should meet."

"Whenever you want."

I had expected an announcement that he could squeeze me in, say, between 5:00 and 5:05 the next day. I had underestimated his edginess. "Know Peter and Paul High over on Cypress? I'll meet you over there in a half-hour. Near the football field."

He hung up before I could say yes or no. I knew the high school field he meant—a square-block expanse with chicken wire fences along only three of the sides. That felt reassuring. If it had been a closed-in area of any kind, I might have been inclined to take a step down Paranoia Path.

As it turned out, Chichester acted as though he had selected his meeting spot to allay suspicions about *me*. When I got out of my car across the street from the football field, I saw nobody until he emerged from behind the wheel of his Lincoln half a block away. Even then he stood still for a moment, waiting to see if anybody was going to jump out of my trunk. Finally, he collected his best pompous stride to go over to the bus station bench in front of the field's fencing. His expensive blue suit and gleaming shoes were Chichester, attorney-at-law; the lack of a tie was a very anxious Chichester, attorney-at-law.

"You're barking up the wrong tree, Finley," he said without preamble, "and that's not going to help you find the animal who killed this boy."

I lighted a cigarette; I had already smoked too many at Chiozza's, but I told myself I was throwing all my excesses into one bag that would be put out with the morning garbage. "Tell me where I'm going wrong, Bob."

He flinched at the "Bob," but gave me my sarcasm. "I want to help. I really do. Nobody needs this kind of sickening tragedy in the papers every day. But you're way off if you think that fire at the Star Video store the other night has anything to do with the death of the Reynolds boy."

"I'm listening."

He seemed to have expected me to be impressed merely by his announcement, and looked stymied for a moment. But then he recovered. "I want to propose an exchange. I think I can provide you with information on that fire . . ."

"I think the word in the penal code is arson."

"Yes, arson. I can give you enough information on that so you'll be completely satisfied it has no direct bearing on the Reynolds boy. From that point, it will be up to you to pursue the question as you see fit. In exchange, I would expect you to desist in these other inquiries you've been making."

"Willy Baker?"

"These other inquiries," he repeated with more emphasis. "Believe me, they won't lead you to Tommy Reynolds's killer, either."

I might have laughed if he hadn't looked so serious—or if I hadn't needed even the marginal scraps he was promising to throw me. "You know so much about who did and didn't kill Tommy, some people might jump to awkward conclusions."

"I'm not here for banter, Finley. My offer is on the table."

Had I underestimated Miles? Had she already started poking into Montauk with Joanna's list? Or had she merely told

Chichester it existed? "If the fire has nothing to do with Tommy Reynolds, why would I be interested in it?"

He nodded. "That's better. The person who perpetrated that vandalism is bent on creating even more confusion than you are. It's in everyone's interests to stop it."

"And?"

"Isn't that enough?"

"Because it's coming from you?"

He sighed in annoyance behind a scan of the quiet street. "I don't know what you think you saw this weekend," he tried again, "but I can assure you you didn't see bad people. They're good people. Some of them are the best this society has. Okay, they let their hair down in what may seem a juvenile way . . ."

"You're about to lose me, Bob."

He wasn't used to juries talking back. "Let me finish!"

"Sure. But let's get to Willy's movies and what else waiters and guitar players are supposed to do for their money."

"Nothing. Absolutely nothing."

"Been a pleasure, Bob."

"Sit down . . . Okay, okay. Sometimes things do happen. Maybe some people go there even expecting little special features. I don't, but others do."

I almost believed him.

"But what are we talking about here? Not the teenagers of our day. I have 10-year-old nephews who understand a lot more about sex than I did at 20."

I didn't give him his smile. "That I know, the penal code hasn't caught up to that revolution."

"And maybe it shouldn't," he said readily. "But you have to see the whole picture. What do these kids see when they go to a house like Baker's? They see money. They see power. Then they see these middle-aged people, some of them desperate for thrills, maybe just dead inside. The kids feel superior. *In their glands,* they feel superior. Whoever comes on to them, that's a pathetic fool. *They're* not going to be like that when they grow up. *They're* lucky. *They've* seen it, know what mistakes not to make with their lives."

"But."

"Exactly. *But.* They're superior and they're lucky, but they're also on this weekend adventure with the local nabobs. And they don't have all the hang-ups you or I might have had at their age. It's the makings for an experience that will make them even more superior, luckier."

"With a few extra dollars in the tip cup."

"That too, if you want to put it that way."

There *was* something in what he was saying—the power question I had asked myself driving Joanna back to her car in Montauk. But because he was saying it as some kind of defense attorney for what he was describing, its value seemed stillborn. "No, I don't want to put it that way, Bob. We're talking about kids, not hookers. I was there when those two girls didn't want to take off their shirts."

"Yes, yes. There's peer pressure too. I'll admit that."

I had known stoned dealers in the overnight tank with a better grasp of a logical flow. I couldn't help wondering how many brain cells he had left home with his tie.

"Some of them think of it as a lark," he said, as though conceding some point to me. "Some of them say no, and that's the end of it. Look, I can't reinvent the wheel for you, Finley. I'm trying to be frank."

"Try harder."

He looked down at his flabby hands as though they had warned him I would be too obtuse to understand. "I'm going to say it again," he said. "Nobody there killed Tommy Reynolds. If I had the least doubt about that, I wouldn't be here. What you and I disapprove of, what society and the law disapprove of, is a separate question."

"Which you'll tackle for the right fee in *your* tip cup."

"Under the right circumstances," he said, trying to look brave for the admission. "But if your interest is the Reynolds boy, that's irrelevant."

What I should have done, of course, was take off from him as fast as I could, run the length of the entire football field with my winning indignation. The problem was, he still had the only thing that promised to be a ball. "I still haven't seen what you're offering."

"The purpose of that fire was to draw attention to Star Video. And not just because Reynolds worked there."

"Because Star Video was a recruitment center for your parties."

"You knew that?"

He looked genuinely perplexed I had tied my own laces without his supervision. Clearly, my reputation wasn't what it might have been. "I hope that's not your only *quid*. How about a name?"

"In exchange for not pursuing those barren trails?"

I could always double-cross him later, I told myself. "A name."

He nodded; far too amenably. "Let's say he was somebody who felt like more of a fish out of water even than you did."

"You can't mean Piccolo."

"Some people are born with advantages. Others don't need them or get along well without them. But then you have still others who never get over seeing themselves as missing out. They'd do anything to change that."

I recognized the Pete Piccolo he was talking about, but that still didn't add up to an arsonist.

"He saw an opportunity," Chichester said, reading my doubts. "Tommy Reynolds worked in the video store, so why not provoke some incident even a nitwit would have to conclude had a bearing on the kid's disappearance? Star Video's records get thrown on the table, familiar names crop up. One little insinuation after another. The fire was one kind of vandalism, but what your employer hoped to cause was a worse kind—discrediting the people he had always wanted to be like."

"Really."

"Really."

"And how does he figure that's the way to ingratiate himself with the people he's so envious of?"

"He's run out of ingratiating tactics, become a little incoherent. Several doors have been closed to him recently, and others will be soon. His impact on a number of people has been distasteful."

I remembered what the Professor had said about the receptionists with a pedigree. "So he burns down Star Video? How did he manage that? I mean, practically. Hide himself in a video box until they closed up?"

"You'll have to ask him that."

"You got to be kidding. This is your evidence?"

"That I'll supply in 24 hours. As you might put it, can I rely on your *pro quo*?"

He was suddenly so cocky I was sure I had given something away. "Mind telling me why I'm such a threat to you? You don't want me sticking my nose into your 'good people,' you have other ways of getting that across besides meeting me here."

I seemed to have hit his funny bone. "Of course. And I'm reasonably sure some calls *have* been made. But I don't want this to get ugly. It would be unnecessary and . . ."

The answer was obvious, of course. "And you don't want to get on the wrong side of Joanna?"

Even the single street lamp was suddenly too bright for him. "I care for Joanna a great deal," he said stiffly. "Enough so I don't want her ever misconstruing what befalls her whims. Is that clear enough?"

It was—and I wished it wasn't. However else he was involved with the Bakers and their taste for kids, I had to admit to myself, Chichester would have never jeopardized his crush on Joanna to be part of anything sticky. Coming right down to it, the two of them were the only ones I could cross off my own list.

"So? Have we a deal?"

"How about I see this evidence of yours first?"

He nodded. "Tomorrow night. Same time here?"

Maybe it was the wind that was blowing up or the lights that had gone out across the street in the last living room, but I didn't want to return to the football field. "Call me at home tomorrow around seven. We'll decide when and where then."

"Fine."

CHAPTER 32

Whatever else had been achieved with my chat with Chichester, I had changed places with him by the time I returned to my car. Now I was the one who was beginning to see goblins hiding in the bushes.

A minute later, I was sure the goblins had passed a driver's test.

It was a dark compact, and it was a good block behind me, but I didn't like the way it hung back there. When I slowed down, it slowed down. I could make out only a driver, but that didn't mean there weren't a thousand clowns hiding in the back seat. I figured I had enough trouble without the clowns.

When I came to the left that would have gotten me home in 10 minutes, I also came to the left that would have brought me to one of the LIRR's more ingenious crossings—a patch of road overgrown with weeds that claimed at least one idiot every year. I wasn't feeling that idiotic, though, so I stayed on the street, one second telling myself I was imagining my pal in the compact, the next second wondering what had happened to the Paul Finley who would have deliberately led the compact to the desolate crossing. The answer to the second thought was easier: That Paul Finley had never existed.

My route took me past the Cameo, now as unlighted as the memorabilia store and the lumber shop. The marquee said it had been a porn night. I got to the main avenue and took a left. There wasn't a single store open, and the night lights were not all that reassuring. But I stopped at the intersection light anyway, figuring

I had about 10 seconds to wait. When the compact came up from the side street, it had little choice but to slide up after me. It was a green Honda. I counted to three, then opened my door.

And really did almost get killed.

My door click in the silent street had been enough for the driver. Lights on full glare, he swerved left and came right for me. I had too many legs to get back into the seat, but somehow I managed to corral them all, throwing the last five or six of them into the air as the Honda sped past. How he missed my door I don't know. How I slammed my left elbow on the knob of the emergency brake I don't know, either. But he did, and I did. By the time I got myself up off the seat again, the Honda had already skidded around the intersection to the right, taking half the asphalt with it.

I had no intention of following. My elbow thought I had done enough merely by sitting up straight and taking a couple of deep breaths: It punished me for so much excess. My consolation, of course, was the knowledge that neither I nor Chichester had imagined our shadow. My heart was so grateful for the vindication it wanted to pump itself right out of my chest.

A head popped out of the door of the chic French restaurant I had checked out after my visit to Boardman. It was a middle-aged woman, and she had the kind of perturbed expression that said something belonging to her had been jangled by the Honda's squealing departure. I was about to assure her I was all right and that, yeah, there was no accounting for the crazy drivers these days, when she skipped the solicitude part and simply closed herself back into the darkened restaurant. Maybe it was just the thought of my pumping blood, but I knew at that moment that was where Joanna had been before she had dropped in on Boardman and *Masters of Peril*.

Pump, pump, pump went my heartstrings.

CHAPTER 33

I woke up the next morning with a throbbing elbow and only the gloomi-
est part of my mind working. The Professor suggested a compress
for the elbow, but wasn't much help for my mind. After he had
digested my adventures with Chichester and the Honda outside
the Coq d'Or, he waved me quiet while he did some scribbling on
a yellow legal pad. For a couple of minutes, I sat obediently at the
kitchen table thinking about nails on blackboards.

"All right," he announced finally. "Want to hear?"

"Have I got a choice?"

"Pour me some coffee. Number one, you give Miles what you
got out in Montauk. Either because of conviction or intimidation,
she doesn't want you sniffing around the Baker set, so she passes
on your information to Chichester directly or to someone aware of
Chichester's interest."

"The latter. Her husband or somebody in the department."

"Check. So now we have all the high and the mighty cursing
the day you dropped in on their party. They've got all these good
moral works to protect outside the local abortion clinic, and that
might look a little hypocritical if they're spending their free time
boffing underage kids. They look into your license and do other
unpleasant things after your meeting with Miles."

"No. They started that crap before. Chiozza told me it's been
going on for a while."

The Professor nodded pensively. "Conclusion?"

"They've been nervous ever since I started pestering them about Tommy Reynolds, not just since Montauk."

"Significance?"

It always came back to the same place. "Piccolo. He's the one who got their wind up about linking the disappearance to Star Video. So, at first they were just working on hypotheticals for dealing with me in case I drew the same straight line. Then the disappearance became an actual murder and then the night of the fire . . ."

"Your ex-partner again."

Despite everything, I hadn't accepted how much of an ex Ellen had become until the Professor made another notation on his pad. "Right. I assumed the customer files were the connection, but just the store itself was enough for them to get antsy."

"Okay. So, then you're a softball star and you nose around in the wrong rooms. Now you're really on their hit list. But first they have to get the Clary kid and the twins to get rid of all that messy evidence."

"No."

"Why not?"

"These people have heard of the telephone, Joe. Why be indebted to Clary and his friends if all they have to do is pick up a phone and tell their managers to get rid of those index cards?"

He had no answer. "Okay, we'll keep that under Open Questions. Now per Chichester last night, the reason they're getting so defensive about everything isn't because of the murder, but because of a fallout scandal. You buy that?"

"I buy it for him. The others . . .?"

"Out with it."

"The whole day out there, I didn't see anything but their fantasies. Their jock fantasies, their sex fantasies. And they certainly didn't look very embarrassed about them."

"Except the wife when she caught you with the tape."

"Yeah, but even that's just housecleaning. Guests shouldn't be looking into broom closets. The fiendishness of serial killers? The telltale furtive look? No, they think they're so beyond daily rules in their little Eden out there, they don't have room for that."

"That can cut both ways. Even a Tommy Reynolds can be forgotten about . . . Well? Is that what you're saying? Yes or no?"

"Thank Christ you were never a cop."

"We're just rolling dice here, Paul. C'mon."

It was Chichester who came back to me again—stalwart, pining Bob Chichester who had his relative values where his circle was concerned and his very absolute values where Joanna was involved. "No."

For some reason, I was relieved when he just nodded and made another note. "Our friend Piccolo," he said relentlessly. "Believe this stuff about the fire?"

"I'll tell you tonight. Why get ahead of ourselves?"

"Why? Because, son-in-law, there are still plenty of hours before tonight, and you seem to be going from one imbroglio to another lately. How about we try to prepare for the next one?"

"Would I believe it of Piccolo? In theory, I suppose. You know him. The only thing worse than losing a game is not being allowed to play in the first place."

"Could he have also killed the boy? "

That seemed like the first easy question he had asked. "No. It doesn't parse, Joe. You're the one who talked to Kimberly about those secretaries and receptionists. What's Tommy Reynolds going to bring Pete? No illusion of self-esteem. Nothing close to that pedigree qualification. He's a leg man and of the opposite sex. He couldn't even be bothered to gape around the batting cage. How's some naked waitress going to help him climb the social ladder?"

"Nobody's that rigidly consistent."

"But if anybody is, it's Piccolo."

He grunted behind a swallow of coffee. "You're not leaving many players on the playing field."

"Maybe Miles is right. Maybe it is the neighbor."

"You really believe that?"

"No."

"But another Open Question, anyway."

"He loved the kid, Joe. He wasn't being phony with me."

"And he goes to Mass every Sunday. Jennifer ever mention her grandfather to you?"

I didn't know where that had come from, and he expected me not to do the oaf.

"He was a regular Augustine. Or so I found out after he was dead. The first part of his life was all bright lights and dark deeds. Then he found the City of God. Not only did he stop his dark deeds, he convinced himself they wouldn't really exist anymore if he didn't talk about them."

What had Gregg—dirty old man Gregg—said when he had seen the condoms in Tommy Reynolds's drawer? *'Is it a sex thing?'*—sounding like an old lady.

"Maybe that's why I fell in love with history. My father hated history. Made him think of his own, I suppose."

"Could somebody like that also not hear what he didn't want to?"

He saw where I was going. "Did Tommy trust Gregg that much to talk openly?"

"He might have. Maybe just some indirect remark to see if the old man might be a help . . ."

"Or another disapproving adult."

"Right."

He took forever to answer. "They never hear what they don't want to hear," he said finally. "You have to repeat it and repeat it and repeat it. But be careful, Paul. Don't accuse him of any-thing. The trick is to get him to volunteer that he's a worldly man who's just been concealing his extra insights into why everything around him is so rotten."

He dropped his eyes to his coffee mug, but didn't touch it. I was glad Jennifer had never gone too far into her grandfather.

CHAPTER 34

Tommy Reynolds was being waked in the largest of the town's three funeral homes. That made sense for accommodating even distant acquaintances attracted by all the publicity, but I also knew it represented one less defense against the total strangers who had nothing better to do than come for a gawk at what they had read about or seen on Eyewitless News. At the wake for Jennifer and Susan, only Lancaster's iron clamp on my wrist had stopped me from clouting a mousy little specimen who had walked up to me with an autograph book.

For once, though, somebody was on the job. Instead of leaving the Visitors book in the wake parlor, someone with a smattering of intelligence had set it up immediately inside the main entrance, where everybody was asked not only to sign his name but state his connection to the deceased. When I walked in, Robinson and another uniform were crowding an elderly woman with purple dye streaks in her hair on how she had become a "friend" of the Reynolds family. When the only answer she could come up with was that she had once lived two blocks away from the Reynolds house, she was escorted back outside and told to send a condolences card.

I wondered if I was going to get the same bum's rush for identifying myself as an "acquaintance." The younger uniform seemed doubtful, but Robinson nodded me inside.

There were 30 or 40 people in the parlor, and half that number again forming conversational huddles in the corridors. Most of the mourners were kids or women who looked like they had thrown a sweater or jacket over slacks between runs back and forth from the supermarket to the washing machine. I didn't have to look at the kids too closely to know Richie Clary wasn't among them.

Mary Reynolds was sitting with a priest on the settee closest to the closed casket. The priest, a carrottop who looked like he doubled as the parish basketball coach, was talking while Mary sat nodding, rosary beads clutched in her tight little hand. A middle-aged couple, looking stiff and vaguely resentful of something, sat on a second settee. I guessed they were the relatives from Pennsylvania somebody had mentioned and I had an inkling of why Mary had preferred raising her brother by herself.

The priest was curious when I walked up and muttered something. Mary took a long moment to recognize who I was (somebody from way back when her brother might have still been alive), then did what she had probably been doing all afternoon—smiled blankly. With that, she dropped her head back to her fist and the beads. The priest gave me a bridge to get away again with something like grace by telling her about cousins in Arizona he had been trying to contact on her behalf.

Gregg and his wife were sitting on folding chairs at the back of the room. That told me that, whatever Miles was trying to pin on him, it hadn't leaked out yet to Mary Reynolds. Better yet, it told me Gregg himself had had no reservations about showing up. As I made my way over to him, I had a picture of Miles and Levine sitting back in the bullpen marveling at how quickly their trial balloon had developed so many holes.

Mrs. Gregg had one of those baggy faces that made me think of people who wanted to be considered cheerful but whose appearance worked against them. She tried not to look suspicious when I asked Gregg to step out into the hall with me. He came only after a start that warned me off ruining his day in front of so many people.

The only niche left not totally overrun was in the smoking lounge. Even there some of the kids had gathered to talk about the bummer of an afternoon they were having, but at least two chairs in the far corner were relatively isolated. I made a point of lighting up in case Robinson or his partner got curious about what I was doing with Gregg. The old fireman watched me with the doomed sense of having to undergo another interrogation.

"There's nothing more I can tell you people," he said as lowly as he could.

I was surprised Miles hadn't informed him of my ranking within the police hierarchy; couldn't she at least have gone through the motions of believing he was the key to the case? "Let me tell you what I think is happening here, Walter," I said, trying to match his modulation. "Some of my colleagues are at a dead end and getting desperate for a suspect. Media pressure, all that crap. They never heard of the past being the past, not when it might help them look good in the present." All the lead he seemed to have been carrying around in his chest and shoulders sagged into his gut as he sat back and sighed. "I know and you know it didn't happen the way they want to believe it did, but unless we can steer them in another direction, they're going to have too much idle time on their hands and they're going to go with their fantasies."

Gregg might have been on Senior Citizen discounts, but he had also dealt with official bodies before. "What makes you so different?"

I remembered the juicer McGowan just in time. "I wouldn't mind sticking it to them. They got me on a leash like I can't be trusted, think they're doing me a favor by letting me keep my shield. But any mistake I've made I don't let it affect my job, the way they are right now."

He nodded. He might have been accused of going after kids, but never of missing a three-alarm bell.

"So what I'm asking you is a very simple thing. I want you to think right now about something—anything—Tommy said to you that you haven't shared with . . . who? Miles and Levine?" (Otherwise known as the Woman and the Jew.)

He didn't need me to remind him of the distasteful. "They don't seem to understand English. I've told them a dozen times . . ."

None of the kids was paying attention to us, but I got up closer to him anyway. "I'm not talking about police crap, Walter. I don't want to hear your alibi, the time Tommy didn't do a good job on the lawn, none of that. We're beyond all that and we're running out of time. What I want you to think about is what you didn't say to Miles and Levine because, frankly, you didn't want to hear it from Tommy in the first place."

It was the first time I wished I had paid more attention to Jennifer's flirtation with books about Zen. I could order my mind only in a very western way to stay blank under Gregg's fearful stare. He was going to flop one way or the other, I told myself not to think, and he was going to make that decision solely based on what he sensed from me.

"Yes," he said at last, a second before the tears started welling up again. "I should have paid more attention. It was last summer. He'd been disappearing on the weekends. When I asked him where he'd been, he'd get this pout like it was none of my business. Never came right out and said it. He was always a polite kid, Lieutenant . . .?"

"Finley."

"Finley. I could tell something was bothering him, but I suppose I thought it was . . . what do they call it? Rites of passage? Not that that alone didn't make me sad. He was always the little boy next door. Dennis the Menace, you know? Guess nobody lives in the comics."

"No."

"That brave little front he kept up after his father and then his mother died. He was the grandson I never had. See, Grace has a problem . . . Well, that's neither here nor there. But the thought of him sneaking into the back of some car . . . Just made me sad."

"Sure."

"There's no middle ground, you see. One day you're one thing, the next day you're out of reach. You may still be polite, and Tommy always tried to be, but it's a different kind of polite. An adult polite. Like you're hiding things instead of just doing what you've been told."

"Last summer, you said?"

He worked the bridge of his nose with a chunky hand until he stopped sniffling. "Yeah, around Labor Day. He was helping me throw out some old luggage from my cellar. Grace wouldn't let me do it without his help. She's convinced I can't bend down for a newspaper without throwing out my back. Anyway, we're in the cellar choking in all this dust. And he starts to talk about a story in the paper about these Chinese or Koreans or something. How they were selling their children to a gangster to get the kids to America. Only it turned out the kids were no better than slaves. Just peddled off and . . . used. Know what I mean?"

"We're adults, Walter. You can spell it out."

He gave me a demerit. "I don't know about these Asians, I told him, but these parents seemed like criminals."

"What did Tommy say?"

"That maybe the kids were smarter than older people gave them credit for. He didn't know what he was saying. Immature, you know?"

"Sure."

"I told him I didn't want to hear that foolishness. There was right and wrong, and those children were being abused. In the eyes of the law *and* in the eyes of God. Where was he getting all these wisenheimer ideas?"

"Where was he?"

Too direct; I almost lost him. But then he came back. "I didn't really want to know where. But he said maybe I was out of touch. Maybe sex stories weren't horrible as some people made them out to be."

"That must have annoyed you."

"Damn right it did. He didn't have the slightest idea what he was talking about. And on top of that, suddenly he's part of the generation that knows everything and we know nothing. Like he's part of some army ready to come crashing through the gates and take over."

Chichester had reacted with mockery and rationalization; I thought I knew how Gregg had reacted, too. "So you slapped him?"

He looked over at the kids, then dropped his eyes again when one of the girls stared back at him. He had drawn so many deep lines on the fake leather armrests they were on the verge of forming a lasting pattern. "Only time in my life I ever raised my hand to him," he said, even his whisper sounding too loud. "Even as I was doing it, I knew I could have stopped my hand if I'd wanted to. But I didn't stop. I got him right under the left eye. He wasn't just being a smartass, Lieutenant. There was *evil* in his eyes."

My cigarette was more ash than tobacco, but I didn't dare give him an excuse to look away. "You don't believe that, Gregg."

"What would you call it?" he charged fiercely. "I know evil when I see it. Even after I'd hit him, he just stood there, like I had done nothing. Like he was on some high ledge looking down on me. Wanting me to admit I was a hypocrite for being so moralistic with him. Like he . . ."

"Knew about your little problem?"

He still wanted to deny it, but then realized he had crossed a line. He nodded as if somebody were pressing his neck up and down. "It was never the same between us after that."

Which still left me nowhere, since I hadn't come to hear about Walter Gregg's mind or soul. "These ideas of his about sex—did you ever get the impression he was talking from personal experience, not just from the gab at the mall or the cafeteria?"

If he had been on an elevator, he would have crash landed into the basement. Now he was too petrified even to look at me.

"Don't run out on me now, Walt. This is the hard part."

"I've just been assuming . . ."

"I understand. And there's all those mixed feelings in there about slapping him. But I need you to go back now to before you thought Tommy was evil."

His tongue searched for something moist on his lips, but didn't find anything. "It was all second-hand, I'm sure about that. He thought he had to brag and act mature with me."

"Brag about what exactly?"

He looked so miserable he could have used the basketball coach consoling Mary. "Movies," he said. "He said he'd heard about people 'having fun' for movies. Nobody got hurt, he said. It was just kids showing off for these rich people. I never heard such talk. These friends of his he was talking about, I couldn't think of them as children, Lieutenant. They liked manipulating sad people."

"But what about Tommy himself? Did he mention anybody specifically he'd been involved with?"

It was too late; he nestled down with his Evil again. "His friends had no morals. It wasn't even sex to them. It was making fun of people who had money to give them. That's not right. Showing your private parts isn't love. That's not even need, is it?"

Grace was standing at the door and looking in at us. Gregg found nothing helpful on my face, then noticed her. He didn't need a better incentive. Without another word, he lifted himself up using both armrests for support and hobbled over to her. She smiled over at me, then heard his grumble and looked more doubtful as they walked out.

I wouldn't need Walter Gregg again, I told myself.

I didn't want to need him again.

Lighting another cigarette seemed like the easiest alternative to returning inside and saying something useless again to Mary Reynolds. What had I accomplished? Taken Gregg's name off the list of suspects? He was as close to having acted fanatically on his notion of evil as he was to multiplying some loaves and fishes. Then again, I had never had him on my list of suspects. As the Professor had said, I wasn't leaving very many players on the field.

CHAPTER 35

By 9:30 that night I knew Chichester wouldn't be calling with his evidence. I told myself he had been too busy to copy the dynamite documents that would pin Piccolo to the video store fire, he would get them to me in the morning. Then I told myself it didn't matter that much anyway, that if everyone agreed Piccolo had nothing to do with Tommy Reynolds's murder, I could live with fewer copies of Tom Cruise movies in circulation. Then I hauled out the telephone directory and looked up Chichester, Robert. There was only one residential listing, for an address in Joanna's Golden Cove district. What had I expected—a tenement in Queens?

"This is Bob," the machine said. "Please leave your name and phone number. I'll get back to you as soon as I can."

The Professor barely looked up when I announced I was going out. He was too busy grousing that the Mets were opening their season in Los Angeles, 10:30 EDT. What would I have said to him, anyway? That I didn't like lawyers screwing around with me? That I didn't like a certain Honda still tooling around out there? That a little fresh air was the best antidote to an attack of the uneasies?

Chichester's place was a colonial on a hilly street with more curves than neighbors. Somebody had once decided it important to build stone walls along the shins of the street as a protection against traffic, but many of the walls were now missing a stone here and there. Did that mean there was a stone shortage or that the only drivers expected to use the road knew the speed limit was two miles an hour?

There was enough grass on all sides of the house to suggest an admiration for Thomas Jefferson, but not quite enough to imagine a patrician. The house was dark, and as I walked up to the front door, I wondered why I hadn't seen any sign of a private security patrol. My ferret returned with some friends when three long rings on the bell didn't bring anybody from inside *or* outside. That was the moment to leave, of course. I did the next best thing by going into my wallet for my favorite Visa card.

The vestibule would have been impressive if I hadn't seen Baker's museum. I felt out of place without a topper and cane to hand to a black servant. But beyond the entrance hall Chichester (or some ex-wife?) had done his best to scale things down to livable proportions. The room to the immediate right of the entrance was some kind of jock room—all the leather and trophies that normally went with Great White Hunters, but instead of animal heads, glassed posters of ancient baseball and football games and tiered cases of bowling, softball, and football awards. There was enough dust in the place to make me think even the cleaning woman came in only once a month. Had I been a little hasty in assuming the guy's yearning for Joanna constituted a healthy sex life?

The next room along the hall was a living room. I didn't bother going in once I noticed the dim light under the door of the third room. A second before I opened the third door, I caught up to my assumption that I didn't have to go through the formality of knocking. And by then my fingerprints were all over the knob.

Chichester was seated in a leather chair in front of a centrally placed teak desk. He was staring up at the ceiling as though something up there had been responsible for the small hole above his right eyebrow. I guessed a .22 and that, rather than from the ceiling, it had been fired from the matching chair eight or nine feet in front of him. Since there was still an odor of cigar smoke, I didn't have to hold my nose against any body stench, but I did anyway in making sure he was as dead as he looked. That fact confirmed, I let it come slowly, piece by piece, the way Dick Geis had once told me he had always done it at a crime scene.

The fat left hand with the $20,000 TAG limp off the armrest.

The fat right hand collapsed in the lap.

Not just cigar smoke, but extinguished cigar smoke, from the ashtray at the edge of the desk near Chichester's chair.

Striped blue shirt without a tie.

Gray pants with a sheen from (house?) wear.

Black loafers.

The only light that of the desk lamp, all the lamps scattered around law library shelves off.

The bottom drawer of the desk on the left not completely shut.

No glasses or other signs of entertaining a guest.

The Rolodex turned to a Wall Street firm, and neatly, as though the killer had just flipped all the cards for obscuring some revealing number.

It rarely worked, but with an old Kleenex from my pocket, I gave the Rolodex a short twist. The card that came up forward was for some engraver—probably the one who had done all the trophy work in the jock room. I went back to the Wall Street firm, then gave the wheel a backward jerk. It was my number.

The ashtray contained nothing but the dead cigar. The ashes were all cigar ashes.

I used my instep to pull out the bottom left drawer completely from underneath. It was a crap drawer—staples, stapler, two box-es of Bics—but with plenty of room for laying a file or folder on top of everything if that was where Chichester had put his evidence.

With the bottom drawer pulled out, I had room to wedge my instep under the middle drawer, as well. It contained nothing but reams of personal stationery. The top left-hand drawer had a keyhole. The pads of my pinkies couldn't budge it: It was locked tight. So were the middle drawer and a cabinet on the right side. I thought about looking for a key, then forgot about it. I was sure that whatever the killer had been looking for, he had found in the bottom left drawer. Why there? Chichester's haste and my pessi-mism. His haste because he had probably just stuck his smoking gun there at the arrival of his unwanted guest. My pessimism because every god in mythology was sticking out its tongue going TOO LATE, FINLEY!

I stood behind the desk a moment open to any thought that would put off closer examination of Chichester himself. Some cops—Lancaster and Miles were two—were very good at antici-pating the findings of the technicals; I never had been. What I had learned at a crime scene, I had usually learned within a few seconds, higher education useless. From where I was standing, for instance, I could see even more clearly that the thin gray and blood tendril snaking down into Chichester's eye had come from a .22. I didn't feel like being any closer.

Then I saw an excuse to put it off. There was an open box with a stack of business cards in the left corner of the desk. The top card said he had sat down at least once recently for a good meal. It was a card from the Coq d'Or.

CHAPTER 36

There was still no sign of a security patrol as I drove back in search of a gas station. I had committed a dozen procedural errors in the house (not even checking out the rest of the premises, for a start), but I concentrated on not committing the one—being traced to a 911 call—that would make the next day truly impossible. I managed it. The Citgo place was still open, so I skipped it for a closed Exxon station another quarter-mile along. I gave the operator Chichester's name and address in my worst Jack Nicholson impression, then hung up.

I had nothing left in front of me except Joanna.

Maybe if I had once won the Publishers Clearing House sweepstakes, I would have been less skeptical about all the coincidences that dropped on me with a thud as I retraced the first part of my flight from Chichester's. The more I thought about the cute distinctions we had made between luck and coincidence, Branch Rickey and Louis Pasteur, the angrier I got. Design and preparation were the themes for my mood, not the luck and chance that were their residue. What exactly had she been up to? And had she been up to it even while we had been rolling around in Chichester's "shack?"

I shut off my head and hit the gas. The nice thing about going into Dick Geis's crime scene mode was that you didn't have to think about what you were seeing, only about what was there to be seen. I had managed that with Chichester, so why not with his dinner companion that Saturday night at the Coq d'Or?

The lights were on full glare in the living room that the maid had kept me out of on my other visit. I slammed my car door as hard as I could. I wanted Joanna running to the window and peering out to see that the Moment of Truth had arrived. Then I stormed up to the door and past the window too fast to see if she did.

She opened the door herself. Surprise and curiosity edged the corners of her eyes. I walked past her before I had to see more. But then a refrigerator closed at the other end of the house. I hadn't planned on that.

"Good seeing you, too."

"Am I interrupting something?"

She became more curiosity than surprise. "That's Hanna," she said, answering my nod to the kitchen. "What's wrong with you?"

One thing less, I told myself, taking in the string of reading glasses around her chest. Wherever the mad thought had come from, I was relieved to get rid of it: *She* hadn't been out in the night with a .22. "Chichester's dead."

She had let go of the front door, and for a second was the cripple she had claimed to be—looking suspended between standing and falling. "No, that's not possible."

"Turn on the radio in a couple of hours and you can hear about it. But we have to talk right now."

Her living room was a well two steps down from the front door. It reminded me of a neatly squared ship. I got down into it before I had to watch any more of her astonishments. I knew they were genuine—and not really enough as that.

"Robert can't be dead."

The opened book on the couch was a novel I had never heard of. The gin and tonic on the table had been only sipped. "Odds are pretty good he was killed by Piccolo."

I hadn't said it before so clearly even to myself. But it was the only thing that made sense. She came down the two steps waiting for me to contradict myself. She might have worn her blue slacks just to make that move down the steps. "I talked to him this morning," she insisted.

"It only happened a couple of hours ago. But I need answers, Joanna. This whole thing's about to blow up in a lot of faces, and one of them could be yours."

"What are you talking about?"

"I think you know more about this business than you've told me. Or maybe more than you yourself realize."

She heard the hope in my voice, too. She lowered herself gingerly to the couch and reached for one of her Marlboros. "I'm not usually unaware of what I know," she said coolly.

"Then convince me. Start with the Cameo."

For a long moment, she had only her cigarette for company as she put Chichester and Piccolo into the roles I had given them for her and found less and less reason to doubt me.

"That night at the Cameo," I tried again. "You went there after you had dinner at that French restaurant around the corner with Chichester. And he told you something that so upset you that . . ."

"Piccolo."

"Excuse me?"

"I wasn't there with Robert. I was there with Piccolo."

It was the truth. Even fundamental logic finally kicked in—kicked and kicked and kicked—to remind me she would have worn heels with Chichester. "With Piccolo," I stumbled on, making it sound like some minor concession. "The two of you had some kind of argument. And it had nothing to do with life insurance payments."

She watched the smoke curl up from her cigarette. I couldn't help agreeing with her: The goddamn cigarettes knew more about what had gone on than I did. "It had everything to do with that money. That was his way of trying to hold on to me."

"You and Piccolo?"

"I told you once—Harold had a very long illness. Months and months of it. Piccolo dropped by a couple of times to see how his money was doing. The first time, let's call it therapeutic. After that . . ."

I got over to the small bar in the corner of the room before I had to show anything. Away from her, I didn't have to toss my understanding and benevolence into the ring to wrestle with my fury. Somewhere in my dim skull, I had even known it. That was why I had gotten so testy with the Professor when he had described Piccolo as the ultimate Lothario. I was accusing *her* of not knowing what she knew? How many other things were swimming around in *my* murk?

"If it makes you feel any better," she said behind me, "I paid for it with interest. After Harold died, I told Piccolo I wanted to put everything behind me, including him. He didn't like that. We had so much in common, he kept telling me. Dragging out the policy payments was his way of staying in my life."

"And you never mentioned any of this to Chichester?"

"After a while. It took some doing. Even lawyers have facial expressions when you tell them certain things. Is he really dead?"

"Yes." I didn't know why I was stinting on the Johnny Walker. I had nothing else to do in the evening except go home and crawl up in a closet. "What happened when you told Chichester?"

"Robert was the closest friend I had. I don't want him dead."

The last thing I needed was her affection for anybody. "What did he do, Joanna?"

"He said he'd take care of it. He did. He came down on Piccolo so hard I had the insurance company check in a week. The creep was afraid of losing his entree to every grocery store in Suffolk County."

"Creep? The little man you put your low heels on for so he wouldn't feel embarrassed by his height at the Coq d'Or?"

She didn't take the bait; she wanted to explain, not fight. "He said it was a peace offering. He wanted to apologize. He hadn't been in his head lately. I guess Harold didn't eradicate all my passiveness."

There was a gigantic oil portrait over the fireplace. A granite block of face. Neatly combed white hair. Sitting on a high stool so he could have his long fingers entwined over his knee and look natural. Harold Mendler had been old enough to be her father, but I couldn't imagine too many people making that mistake. *Nothing*, not even generations, came after him.

"He picked me up and took me to that restaurant. He was proud it was his discovery. Classy, but not patronized by people like Robert because they thought anything in town was beneath them. He actually said that. When we sat down, I suddenly didn't know what I was doing there. I couldn't look at him. I despised him so much. He went on about this and that, but all I could think about was how I'd let him manipulate me. I despised him and myself. He'd made me feel as ugly as Harold Mendler had made me feel smart, able to take care of myself. Over and over he kept saying we were both outsiders and how that would always be a bond between us.

"Finally, I just got up and walked out. Madam Polite. Know what I did, Finley? The woman who ran the place, she was so shocked I'd leave without eating that I took a card from the counter to show her I'd be back and bring all my friends. Bring Robert and the Bakers and all the other people Piccolo couldn't stand. Then he'd have no secret place to eat, either!" She reached for her gin, but then changed her mind and took another puff, instead. "I looked for a taxi, but I didn't really want to come back here or walk or anything. I went to that movie just to get off the street before he came after me. When I had enough of those men changing their seats to get near me, I got up to leave. I told myself enough time had passed; Piccolo had left the restaurant and I could go back there and call a cab. That's when I fell. I wanted to stay on that floor forever. Until somebody came to cart me away. I belonged on that floor, with all those slimy people stepping over me. I could even believe it was my fault Harold had suffered so much."

"But you got up."

"I got up. And that delightful Boardman came along to make it sound like I'd come in just to soil his furniture. It was the last straw. In the restaurant, Piccolo had been going on about how Gramercy Insurance was carrying every business in town, including the Cameo, and how that made him somebody of substance or something." She glanced up at Mendler. "He doesn't have a clue."

I thought of two-way streets: Not only what Mendler had given her, but how she must have fed the old man's ego. As she had fed mine only two days before.

"It came out like vomit. Whatever it took, I was going to hurt him. Robert wasn't enthusiastic, but he went along when I threatened to go to somebody else. I know what he was thinking. Keep it in the family. Wait for the hysterical woman to calm down. Maybe he was right. All I was up for was to see Piccolo knocked on his ass. I wanted *him* in the aisle of that movie house. You came close. Thank you."

I warned myself against parsing *close*.

"He really killed Robert?"

"He probably showed up unexpectedly at Chichester's. Chichester tried to calm him down, get him to sit down and have a reasonable chat . . ."

"Robert detested him."

"General principles or because of you and him being together?"

"Both."

"If you had to . . ."

"If I was so horny, why not Robert? You still don't listen very closely, do you? Robert is . . . was a gentleman."

"Who loved you."

"I wasn't looking for love. I already had that. Didn't I say that?"

There was still one person missing from the story, I realized—Tommy Reynolds. "Before you ran out on Piccolo, you said he was going on about this and that. About Tommy Reynolds?"

"The policeman rises again."

"The policeman retired. I haven't."

"He didn't mention Tommy Reynolds."

"For Christ sake, Joanna, nobody's that much in hock to a one-night stand!"

It was out and was even uglier aloud than it had been wafting around in the recesses of my mind. "What are you accusing me of?"

"Of too many coincidences. Maybe just of me!"

I was drinking her liquor, standing on her rug, using up her living room air: I had seen the look in some nightmare. But then she tried once more to forgive me. "You're right," she said. "Nobody's that much in hock to a one-night stand. It takes years of self-hatred, of feeling sorry for yourself. It takes opening your eyes in the morning and thinking to yourself right away that everything's been a big cheat, but at the same time maybe not enough of a cheat. It takes every single doubt you've ever had about yourself, but that somebody let you forget for a while. Now he's dying and you're back to where you started. The glorified receptionist with a ton of money, but still the glorified receptionist eager to do everybody's bidding, taking my pants off the least of it. It takes everything you are."

That still wasn't enough. I could have walked out then just to leave her alone, but it still wasn't enough.

Only it wasn't my decision.

"Goodbye, Finley," she said, finally reaching over for her drink.

CHAPTER 37

I drove around for more than an hour. I had nothing better to do, and Paul Finley, Private Investigator certainly didn't. I took block after block of two-story homes, making the sociological observation that the bedrooms were probably upstairs and the kitchens downstairs. I thought about typing up my findings and sending them to some serious academic journal. I got on the highway for a while so I could include gas stations, fast food franchises, and parking lots in my study. I decided the gas stations sold gas, the fast food franchises fast food, and the parking lots dented fenders.

I almost made a mistake by turning on the radio, ending up in the middle of a third-inning rally by the Mets against the Dodgers. I pressed the button for QXR before I heard the score. Whatever the score was, I knew it. QXR cooperated to the fullest by playing Mozart or Billy Joel, one of those tinny Muzak guys.

At one point, I passed a squad car, figuring it was probably the only one in the county not at the Chichester house. I liked picturing the consternation on Miles's face when she heard the news and liked, even more, the stark fear that would overtake her husband when she told him about it. Chichester hadn't been the captain of the ship, more like a chief steward, but the boiler room would be taking on water for the next few days.

All of us had our Titanic dreams, right?

I was almost to the Queens line when my ferret family appeared. Nobody wanted to roam as far as Queens, they warned—so there, a gnaw of your nerves. Put my head back together. Figure out where the next curve might come from.

They had a point, so I turned back toward the house. I gave myself until the end of the drive to work out my next move.

Most immediately, there was Piccolo wandering around somewhere with a gun. He had to have been; he had been acting desperately too often lately.

Rash judgment? I didn't think so. It had to have been him—tonight at Chichester's and last night in the Honda that had followed me from the football field. So, Piccolo down. But how did I persuade Miles to get him out altogether?

With the truth, of course. There was the consolation I had been angling for: *Cover-up time was over*. No way they could collar Piccolo for Chichester without having everything else come out, too. Everybody was going to end up with a singed ass.

Unless Piccolo blew his brains out.

The possibility straightened me up behind the wheel. The pathetic son of a bitch couldn't kill himself, I wouldn't let him. It would have been too convenient for everybody. Goodness and Justice were riding on his being arrested and telling his smarmy tale to a jury. *I* was riding on it.

I didn't recall his exact address, but I knew I would recognize the house. Two years ago, the Professor had fallen and sprained a knee coming down the stoop after one of our fantasy league meetings. I had stood on those steps a good 20 minutes waiting for the old man to say he could walk and joining Stedina, Chiozza, and the others in needling Piccolo about his home liability insurance. Now that I thought of it, he hadn't contributed a penny to the Professor's medicinal bandages.

The Dodgers had scored a run. Gary Cohen insisted it was a lucky run—two tricklers and a broken-bat sacrifice fly. That wasn't the point, I wanted to scream at him through the radio. Lucky run or not, it shouldn't have been scored. We had finished with residues.

Piccolo wasn't home. Every window was darker than dark. The mail was sticking out of the postal slot in his door. The garage was sealed tight. If I hadn't been looking for him to stop him from killing himself and to accuse him of murder and arson, I might have lectured him on telltale invitations to burglars.

I didn't expect him to hole up in his office, but I took that route home anyway. The Gramercy Insurance building didn't show a single light outside that on the desk of the lobby guard. The guard reminded me of the turnover in Gramercy receptionists and why I still didn't buy Piccolo as the killer of Tommy Reynolds.

I went home. And found Pete Piccolo.

CHAPTER 38

He was sitting in the corner of the couch, the same seat he had taken for our first draft. Instead of heaps of player statistics on his lap, though, he had the .22 every cop on the Island was hunting for.

"Where you been, Finley?"

I looked over to where the Professor was masticating on the unusual puzzle at hand. He was afraid, but not much more so than he would have been if a student had challenged him about the accuracy of some date he wasn't 100 percent sure about. The game was on the TV, but without sound.

"I was just telling Joe we don't need an announcer," Piccolo said, brandishing the zapper. "We can see what we can see, right?"

I thought of a jumper named Mitchell who had once gotten to the roof of his office after being fired from some sales job. Except that Mitchell had been threatening only himself. "You look pretty worn out, Pete."

"Yeah, well." He looked off at the screen. Even that minuscule movement seemed to push the big knot of his tie into his Adam's apple. He had worn his natty three-piece brown suit even to kill Chichester. "What we got here, Joe? Still 2-1?"

"I think so."

"Why don't you give me that thing, Pete?"

"I did something stupid tonight, boys. I panicked."

I ignored the Professor's look to accent the positive, as I had with the jumper Mitchell. "None of it has to do with Tommy Reynolds. What's the sweat?"

Misstep. His smirk told me I should have paid attention to the Professor's glance. "Oh, c'mon, Finley. You've been to see Chichester. He didn't call like he was supposed to, and you went to find out why. Isn't that what you said, Joe?"

"Not exactly. All I said was . . ."

A loud groan. "God, I hate academics! They can't even do an actuary table without throwing in the New Mexican Indian who was exposed to the black plague. Okay, you just *assumed* that's where he was going. So how was Bob, Finley? He give you what you wanted?"

"You know he didn't. You were there first."

"Have you figured out what this McGuffin was?"

I didn't mind him toying; it not only gave me time but said he wasn't all that sure what he wanted to do. "He said it would prove you were behind that mall fire."

"Yeah? So, what is it?"

In for a penny. "One of two things, I'd say. A letter to him or somebody else admitting you did it . . ."

"Do I look like that much of a jerk?"

"Then I'd guess it's a statement from whoever helped you, the person who actually started the fire. Sure as hell, it wasn't you."

He was impressed, and I agreed with him. I *was* a genius—now that I was about to be blown away.

"Go ahead. Who's this torch man?"

"I'm sure you've run across a few professionals in your job."

He scowled, no longer impressed with me. "Christ, maybe I've been overpaying you. But that's water under the bridge. The question before the panel is what comes next."

"If you have this evidence," the Professor piped up, "it ends there. What's the problem?"

"Tell him, Finley. Tell him what the problem is."

When I did, the Professor said only "Oh, I see," then took his first clear look at the game.

"He sees! Hallelujah! What would you have done, Joe? Here's a guy knee-high in mud but with a nice homburg on his head, and *he's* telling *me* I'm finished! That I've always been an outsider and now I'm about to become something even worse—an insider in a prison cell. Suppose some college bigwig told you that? What would you do?"

"Tell him to go fuck himself," the Professor said promptly.

"That's all, huh?"

"Yeah, that's all."

Piccolo leaned forward so abruptly the Professor flinched. "But he could have ruined me. And with the help of your son-in-law here."

"The only thing I've been interested in is Tommy Reynolds. Did you kill him?"

"You know I didn't."

"No, I don't really."

The gun came up, and I was sure I had blown it. I didn't need to remember that Mitchell had attempted a header from the roof and that, for all my tactics, a fireman and Levine had been the ones to save him with last-second grabs. "Where do you get so much fucking arrogance, Finley? Just because you kicked me out of bed with the ice queen?"

"She seems to think she kicked you out."

"Fuck you!"

"Look at your situation, Pete. The arson is penny-ante now. They're looking for you for homicide. How do you get out of that one? Killing us, too? I don't think so. Then you'd have to kill your torch too, wouldn't you? I mean, if he was willing to play ball with Chichester, he'll sure as hell cooperate with the cops or the DA. You got a mountain of shit, pal, and you're only making it higher for your fall."

The gun wavered, and for a second I thought he was going to go for the Professor first and that I would have to spring at him anyway. But then he put it back in his lap. "I didn't want it like this."

"Who would?"

He was oblivious to staring into the lamp next to him, to his vision being splotched. "When I broke up with Jan," he said, "I wanted to think it was about money. But it wasn't. The guy she's married to now doesn't make half what I do. Know what she really wanted, Finley? She wanted us to be *above* money."

I had never met his wife and didn't think I had to for doubting what he had convinced himself of.

"People like Baker, they have money. But what separates them from other people is they're above it, too. I could never give Jan or the kids that. Every time we'd go to my family in Brooklyn for the holidays, I wanted her to see how better off we were than my old man the baker. He himself would tell her that. But that was never enough for her. We'd barely get home and put the kids to bed, and she'd start in about how low I seemed to be aiming. About how it seemed enough for me to be making more than my old man."

"Maybe she just didn't like you being so presumptuous toward your father."

"Who the hell are you—a marriage counselor now? I know what she meant. She wanted me above my old man, not just ahead of him!"

The Professor leaned out of his seat to break Piccolo's attention, and it worked. "What do you want?"

"The remote control. I want some sound on the game."

One diversion, two diversion: "And you really thought burning down that video store was going to get you somewhere?"

He snapped his head back to me. For a moment, he had only clutter in his hands—a gun here, a zapper there. "It got them to come out of the woodwork, didn't it?"

"Against you. That some kind of victory?"

"They didn't have to react that way."

"Christ Almighty, Pete, of course they did!"

"Like hell! Once you started nosing around . . ."

"*Me?*"

"Of course you. Star Video's on Gramercy's books. Think I would've given that claim to anybody else? You're the one who ruined it by showing up out at Montauk Sunday."

My joints felt like they were leaking sand. "Ruined what, exactly?"

He couldn't understand how so much stupidity could be standing in the same room with him. "You were going to be my message to them, Finley. They wanted to keep treating me like shit? Get even Joanna against me? Fine. But let them try to pull you off the Star Video case. I had a lot of confidence in you, fella. You'd have gotten to the core of everything, no hidden political agendas to stop you. They *had* to come to me in the end."

Where did I start? By pointing out that if Finley the Invincible had been so Invincible, what he would have found at the core of everything was Piccolo the Arsonist and that this might have been very counterproductive to getting back on a Montauk softball field? I didn't waste my time. What seemed more to the point was that I was looking at a lunatic and the lunatic had been looking at me as the solution to all his social problems.

"Come on, Finley. Admit it. It could have worked."

Humor the loon, my nod said. But then I didn't want to nod anymore—to him or Joanna or Chichester or to all the other deliverers of Truths Finley Has Overlooked. "You mean, try to get through extortion what you couldn't get by fucking your way into their circle."

In the Professor's place, I too would have been astonished, would have thought I *wanted* Piccolo to shoot. But Piccolo didn't shoot. He was too furious for anything so logical. It took forever for me to realize he was jumping up to charge me. The coffee table gave me one precious second, the Professor's big foot another. Piccolo didn't hit me so much as stumble into me.

And I blew it.

I was so worried about the gun still in his hand that, instead of aiming my fist squarely into his face, I whacked out too fast, clipping him only on the side of the head. It didn't stop him. Too many hours of squash, jogging, calisthenics, and dieting had gone into the boulder that drove into my chest and knocked me against the wall. Even then I had eyes only for the gun. I don't know how many head butts and left hands with the edge of the zapper he got in as I grabbed his right wrist and tried to keep the gun nozzle pointed up or just away.

His right wrist finally gave, and I heard the gun hit the carpet. The bad news was that this left both his hands free, and he knew how to use his reinforcements better than I knew how to use mine. All my second hand seemed good for as he clamped down on my throat was knuckling his shoulder blade. I could already feel the swooning darkness coming when the Professor's hairy forearm came across Piccolo's eyes. The old man was grunting and grunting, but his forearm was enough. Between his tugging and my finally liberated right knee, Piccolo was down on the floor.

And back next to the gun. I was dead. The Professor was dead. The world was dead. That was all there was to say.

So why didn't we all die? Even when I saw through my blurred eyes that Piccolo was scrambling for the door, I was sure he would turn around at the last second and fire back at both of us. But he didn't. He was raving and crying and cursing, but most of all he was running, a wild dog loose in the neighborhood.

The Professor took forever to sit up on the floor. He couldn't gasp loudly enough, his face was red and white, and blue might have been coming. "Call the cops," I managed.

I pushed myself out to the kitchen and downstairs to the basement. We were in High Throb time in my chest, around my throat, and at the back of my head, but I didn't dare wait for a next wave that might have put me down for good. For some reason, my .38 and clip were sitting in the file cabinet drawer where they should have been. I thought that the most freakish development on the evening as I tried to get back up the cellar steps without killing myself. The old man was still sitting on the floor in the living room as though he had earned his daze and had no further obligations.

"Call them, for Christ sake!"

"Yeah, yeah."

Piccolo was about a block away, just tramping down the corridor of hushed homes, his gun loose in his right hand. He was crying something, but so far nobody had been curious enough to look out and ask him what he wanted.

Wrong.

Even as I was deciding to go after him on foot rather than take the car, a kid in a sweatshirt stuck his head from an upstairs window and shouted down for him to shut up. Piccolo stopped, took a long second to track down the source of the command, then simply fired up at the window. The kid dove back out of sight as the crack disturbed a couple of pigeons in an eave.

And on he went. By the time I got to the kid's house, a down-stairs light had come on. And then another from the house direct-ly across the street. Small favors, I told myself: Now it wouldn't be entirely up to Joe to call the cops.

Piccolo was wandering nowhere, but wandering nowhere fast. He was all but jogging. Even in his three-piece suit and craziness, he was going to get to the boulevard before I could stop him. Was it so important to stop him before the boulevard? I told my lungs it was, that I didn't want him firing at the traffic there. Who cared about the goddamn traffic, my lungs replied reasonably enough; wasn't it already bad enough he was endangering the people on the block? No, said I; the people on the block should have been in bed, they deserved to be shot if they looked out their windows.

And then he helped again. With less than half a block to go before the boulevard, he slowed down, took a wide, staggering step, and turned back to me. The tie had come out from under his vest, but the knot still looked like it was gagging him.

"You're out of shape, Finley!"

I stopped short. One final lesson from some academy teacher. I could reach him with my .38, but there was no way in hell—per the manual—he could reach me with his popgun. "Give it up, Pete!"

He thought that was funny. He gazed around at the dark-ened windows to see if they agreed. Out of the corner of my eye, I thought I saw somebody opening a screen door. "Look around you, Paul! I bet we have millions tied up on this street alone! Life, fire, burglary! What do you think?"

"Auto, too! A regular Gramercy industry!"

Too condescending. He was more interested in me again. "There was no future for you with Gramercy, anyway," he said, sounding sane and mean again. "You know that, don't you? You would've done that final favor for me, then you would've been expendable. That's the way the Chichesters operate. Sorry to say it, but you wouldn't have been much of a price to pay."

There were voices behind me—almost a block away, but near enough. "I was getting a little stale anyway, Pete. How about put-ting that thing down?"

"*You* were getting stale!!! The whole business is on its last legs, for Christ sake! Accidents alone. Microwaves instead of open skillets. Plastic forks so you can't slit your friend's throat. Plastic chairs so you don't fall and break your back. Claims are coming down in that category so fast . . . Ah! What the hell do you care? You don't know what insurance is. You think it's all about some incompetent dentist."

I calculated five more feet before I was within his range. "We can work all this out, Pete. You've been upset lately. I can lead the parade of witnesses about that. I mean, just the way you were bidding on Barry Bonds in the draft . . ."

The .22 came up so fast I had time only to think he was piling one more futility atop all his others. I even saw the discarded candy wrapper about where his bullet should have parachuted down short of me.

Except it didn't. My left arm turned on me so hard it was like a ferret convention. I staggered against a parked car, my arm yelling and flapping and singing so hard I almost cracked my jaw on the car's rearview mirror. There was a heavy slam of the screen door in a house behind me. Then another cry from up the block to call the police.

"You didn't earn your money, Paul. You blew it by going to Montauk, showed all our cards too soon."

I aimed for the tie knot. It seemed to have been there for that purpose forever. My first shot missed, but the second didn't. He didn't even have time to clutch at what was wrong. He just fell backward and down.

I counted to three without moving. What academy asshole had told me I would have been in the clear from a .22 from my distance? I thought of a few names, then inched forward. There was so much blood over Piccolo's shirt and vest I wondered if that was the river waiting to explode inside me, too.

"Great shot, man."

I wasn't in the euthanasia business, and wanted to kill him for the sarcastic insinuation I shouldn't have been.

"But one-for-two still leads most leagues."

"What the fuck did you shoot for?"

He had no answer to that, so dismissed the question. "I was exaggerating before," he said. "There'll always be a call for robbery insurance. Know my old man?"

I could feel without seeing people approaching warily behind us. "A baker, you said."

"In Bensonhurst. Even he's been robbed."

I turned back to see six or seven people creeping toward us. They were so ridiculous in their stealth they reminded me of those evil trolls in *Babes in Toyland*. "Somebody call an ambulance!"

"Fuck them. Listen to me, Finley. Know what they took from my old man? Sixty-seven dollars and five coconut custard pies! Even the fucking coconut custard pies have to be insured!"

I knew his rales meant it was too late even for an SST ambulance. "Tommy Reynolds, Pete. I must know. Was it you?"

The coconut custard pies melted out of his eyes. There was nothing but panic as he tried to grab me. I leaned lower to be grabbed, even if it was my arm. "They're going to blame me for that, Finley! Don't let them do that! Make a detailed report and get your best typist on it! Okay?"

He didn't have any more strength to grab. His hand fell back on his stomach and died like the rest of him.

"Okay," I said.

CHAPTER 39

Even without my minor arm wound and a cracked rib, they would have probably found some plausible reason for penning me in a hospital room for three days. As it was, the whole county was ostensibly showing its gratitude to me for taking a madman off the public thoroughfares by insisting I have round-the-clock care to head off potential medical complications. The local newscasts were filled with the same gratitude, with everyone from the County Executive to the man on the street agreeing that Paul Finley had been there when he had been needed. The parade of doctors and nurses into my private room was also mostly celebratory since anything professional that had to be said and done about my condition had been said and done by the ER doctor the night of the shooting. On the other hand, my fans in white and scrubs got decidedly evasive when I asked why none of the reporters who were telling my life story in the papers and on the tube had been allowed in for a first-hand interview. All that question got me was advice to take another nap.

My only visitor was the Professor. Any hopes for stirring the pot through him were dashed by his escort—a trim little man with a potato head from the prosecutor's office named Alderson. Alderson's idea of saying hello was to remind both of us that the investigation into the killings of Tommy Reynolds and Robert Chichester had entered "an extremely delicate stage," so it was our duty to "assist the process." To be sure we assisted the process, he stood by the window for the Professor's 15-minute visit, trying not to look suspicious whenever we mentioned some rookie third baseman he had never heard of. I could see from the Professor's eyes he was up for a little trouble with the reporters as soon as he left me, but I discouraged him. I had no doubt that if Alderson anticipated the slightest awkwardness, he would have immediately recommended hospitalizing Joe as a potential stroke victim.

In short, Piccolo had called it with his dying breath: He and he alone was going to take the fall for everything. And for three critical days, I could do nothing about it but watch it unfold on television and in the papers. Initial indications became unofficial reports. Unofficial reports became the views of reliable sources. The views of the reliable sources evolved into the findings of investigators. And finally, the investigators were holding a press conference and confirming everything. Miles had never looked so authoritative than when she stood next to the County Executive, his chief aide McDonough, Police Chief Rimini, and Lancaster to announce there was sufficient evidence to say that an overwrought Peter Piccolo had raped and slain Tommy Reynolds after the boy had rejected his advances and had then sought to cover up his heinous crime by first torching Star Video to remove any trace of his patronage of the store and by then shooting Robert Chichester, who had become suspicious of Piccolo's irrational behavior. The Montauks? Willy and Cecile Baker were beside themselves with grief at the thought that Piccolo had hit on Tommy Reynolds only because the pervert had met the boy as a waiter in their home the previous summer.

Then there were the side dishes. Richie Clary telling reporters he had been aware of Piccolo's advances toward his friend Tommy the previous summer but had thought it had ended there. Mary Reynolds, her hands looking naked without rosary beads, shaking her head and saying she hoped Piccolo would be judged by "a just God." Jan Butler, Piccolo's ex-wife, being hounded out of a supermarket by reporters until she finally turned around and told them to go bleep themselves.

Maybe I should have been disgusted, but I was mainly fascinated. I couldn't get enough of every single rock of the avalanche rumbling down the mountain and covering Piccolo up a little more. Anger? Twice, I suppose. The first time was when I heard Miles blithely using my old suspicions about Star Video's customer records as the motive behind the fire. The second time was when Mary Reynolds was dragged on to do her bit. Beyond that, though, I couldn't afford a simple thing like anger. As far as official and influential Nassau was concerned, I didn't need reminding, I was still a loose cannon. They couldn't keep me in a hospital room forever, so, aside from the obvious threats to my license, they had to be planning something far more direct for Paul Finley. That prospect provided far too much food for thought to be detoured by anger (or by an odd thought here and there that Joanna could have at least called). It even made me hesitant about the meals the Jamaican ladies delivered punctually three times a day. I didn't like the idea of not being around to read the headline: HERO INVESTIGATOR CHOKES ON PINEAPPLE CHUNKS.

But I ate. And groused about how final Joanna's "Goodbye, Finley" had been. And watched more television than I had watched in 10 years. When there weren't newscasts praising me and Miles or "analyzing" Piccolo's demented background, there were the Yankee opener and reruns of old cop shows. I had never noticed before how even the worst of the cop shows had gotten some obscure procedural detail absolutely right. I was impressed. Until then, the only cop show that had ever seemed even mildly real had been "Barney Miller." But several hours a day from my bed, I felt like an eavesdropper on snatches of precinct talk and behavior I might have actually been exposed to on the job. When some of the programs went wrong, it was usually because they tried to be too smart, over-scheming when simple scheming would have been enough. Like teenagers.

It was a criticism I chewed on my last night in the hospital while I tried to fall asleep within the unnatural silence of a public building. And then the thought I had been keeping in the back of my mind for a very long time popped out in crystal clarity: *Richie Clary had killed Tommy Reynolds.*

CHAPTER 40

There was so much cheerfulness from the two floor nurses as I got dressed to check out that I couldn't wallow in the hangover that had descended on me while sleeping. I also could have done without their dumb looks when I asked if the Professor had arrived to take me home. The big blonde named Clancy said something like she was "sure" he had had trouble parking and was waiting downstairs in front of the entrance. As I was wheeled downstairs to Administration, that was enough of a vague answer to make me the sure one—that Miles was lurking nearby to drop the second shoe. On her official visit the first night to get my version of the Piccolo shooting, she had already looked anxious to deliver the message from the gods. Why had she held her fire then? I supposed it was because she had yet to integrate my verbal into the fiction being prepared in Mineola. Now that the paper house had gone up, though, there was nothing to stop her from reminding me personally that no tramps would be allowed.

Once again, I was wrong. It wasn't Ellen Miles who was waiting for me under the entrance canopy, but Gil Stedina. "There you are!" he said merrily, grabbing my bag from my good hand. "You don't look the worse for the wear!"

In his mall security uniform, Stedina looked like buckled fat; in his windbreaker and jeans, he looked like just fat. "Where's Joe? He said he'd pick me up."

Stedina tossed my bag into the back of his blue Nissan. "Guess he got the times mixed up. That good enough or you want more bullshit?"

I didn't want more bullshit, but I did want more than his Let's-Be-Smart-Men-of-the-World smirk. I found it in two interns coming out of the automatic glass doors behind me; one's nametag said PATEL, the other's SHINER. "Hey, you're Patel and Shiner, right?"

The Indian thought I had escaped from the psych ward, but Shiner recognized me. "Paul Finley!"

"You got it. And I just want you guys to know for the record that my good friend Gil Stedina has dropped by to pick me up today. That's him there. And we're using his blue Nissan. Tell them, Gil."

Stedina liked himself for being a good sport, flipped the car keys in his hand, and got behind the wheel. I hadn't realized before that two good arms were essential for getting in a car smoothly. Patel and Shiner were still looking after me curiously as we pulled away.

"You're getting paranoid, Finley."

"No, I'm not. People really are after me. Left here."

Naturally, we went right. "A little detour. There's someone who wants to see you. Just for a couple of minutes."

"The Wizard himself?"

"It's a situation. Just don't ask me questions I can't answer."

"You used to ask a lot of questions, Gil."

"That was then."

He started following signs to Baldwin and Oceanside. At least we weren't going to the Golden Cove and I wouldn't be stunned to discover that Joanna had been running the Evil Empire between her Cameo falls.

"So what're we going to do about Piccolo's players?" Stedina asked, more relaxed to be on the highway. "Okay, it's not the nicest thing to worry about, but he's got Bonds and a couple of others. Should we throw them back in a common pool, have another draft, what?"

It was the first time in three days I even felt capable of laughing. I took one of his cigarettes from the dashboard as a reward. "Give me a light. I'll ponder that problem on the way to the Wizard."

He looked miffed as he took a Bic out of his shirt pocket and gave it to me. Instead of deliberating on the fate of Piccolo's draft picks, I parsed the idea of Gil Stedina on the circuit. He could fetch and carry, but so could a hundred other ex-cops. Why was he more trustworthy than, say, Miles for conveying the atomically ticking package known as Paul Finley?

And then I knew why and did laugh. Not a happy laugh or a merry laugh, but a laugh. "*You* set that fire! You're the one Piccolo hired!"

He took his chauffeuring assignment too solemnly to take his eyes off the road. "I think all that stuff's settled, isn't it?"

"It had to be you! You had the keys to the place! Jesus, Gil!"

"They must've doped you up pretty good in that place."

Even Piccolo's ravings in those final seconds suddenly fit. "And I bet he didn't promise you just money, either. Somebody with your background should have something better than rattling door locks every night. I know, Gil! How would you like a steady gig with Gramercy Insurance?"

He had to admit I was funny. "Way I heard it, you weren't going to be there much longer anyway."

It was nice to know Piccolo hadn't been lying about planning on throwing me over the side. It was even nicer knowing that I had more than a torch man next to me. "So why'd you turn on him?"

"You're fishing, buddy."

"Like hell. You were the torch man and you were Chichester's evidence, too."

He couldn't swing over to the right exit for East Bay fast enough. "Water under the bridge," he said tightly. "You make mistakes, you get into situations, you hope you can get out of them. Now do me a favor and save up that talking you want to save up."

It was as much as I was going to get from him, but the rest wasn't hard to work out. Miles or the fire marshals had reached the conclusion of an inside job and gone to Freed or Freed's bosses with the usual questions about disgruntled employees. The questions had gotten back to Chichester and the other Star Video investors, someone had remembered a tidbit about Piccolo and Stedina socializing in a fantasy league, and Stedina had been approached for another round of questions. His call: Did he want to be charged with arson or help resolve a sticky situation for one and all?

"Piccolo was crazy," he suddenly blurted. "How come it took you so long to see it?"

Only one answer occurred to me immediately: He had been nice to me at the right time.

CHAPTER 41

We didn't exchange another word into East Bay. There were a few boats in the harbor, but ten times as many gulls creaking and diving for garbage. We ended up at a modest bungalow about five minutes' walk from the main harbor; there was a new black Range Rover parked in front. I got out of the car, but Stedina stayed put. I took a deep whiff of sea air and went over to the door.

I couldn't deny being flattered to see that my host was the man who liked to be known as the Governor, even though he had covered that job for less than a year. He was drinking coffee at a picnic table in a far corner of a spacious main room. He looked paunchier than in recent photos, but even seated he was the leggy, prematurely gray man who had once been filmed regularly walking into street crowds and banquet rooms with a sober smile for those who would one day elect him to the White House. He hadn't made it, but he had made even his failure seem like a defect of the system and a shortcoming of those who went along with it.

"Thank you for coming, Mr. Finley. May I pour you a coffee?"

For memorable pourers, he beat any counterman at Wendy's. Close-up, his lumberjack shirt seemed like a bad idea: He had more need than ever of a dress shirt and tie to cover the loose skin around his throat.

"Still stings a little, I imagine," he said, taking in my sling as I tried to get comfortable across from him.

"More than a little."

He nodded, but once he had set the coffee and a pewter sugar bowl within my reach, he had exhausted the niceties. "I'm sure you've had your fill of compliments you're a little uneasy about. The fact is, this sordid affair has done nobody any good. Bob Chichester was a good friend. I'm confident I'm speaking for him in saying we have his assassin and we should move on to other things. Do you agree?"

I had expected to be able at least to sip my coffee before I spoiled the day. "We have his assassin. No question."

He was already disappointed in me. "Meaning?"

"Pete Piccolo killed Chichester and he was behind the video store fire."

"There were motives behind those frenzied acts."

I got a sip before I was shown the door; it tasted like the cheapest ground. "But not the murder of Tommy Reynolds. Pete Piccolo didn't do that."

He showed nothing. "It certainly seems to fit."

I was annoyed I hadn't grabbed one of Stedina's cigarettes. "So I keep hearing, Governor. But I think we both know what happened."

"We do?"

"Richie Clary and Tommy Reynolds went into those woods together. They got into an argument. I don't know about what, maybe something to do with Tommy wanting to tell somebody about Baker's softball weekends. And Richie picked up a rock and killed him."

He tried to look amused, but also seemed to be making an effort not to look somewhere. There were two closed doors leading to the rest of the house, and I suddenly knew we weren't alone. "Speculation, Mr. Finley, and pretty grisly speculation."

"Granted. But that's what happened. And then Richie stripped the body to make it look like a sex attack. It's the kind of thing you can learn sitting at home and watching prime time. I learned a few things myself last night from a hospital bed."

"Oh? What were they?"

"Watching some of these cop shows. I was reminded how teenagers tend to be too elaborate about things they're trying to cover up. Like a day I followed Richie Clary around while he took some index cards out of video stores. A friend of mine asked why he would have done something like that if not because somebody asked him to. The reason is that he thought he was being clever. Your typical teenage monologue delivered to the not-so-clever world."

He shifted in his seat, as though he wanted his shoulders as a more pronounced wall to one of the doors. "And are you also suggesting the Clary boy committed this obscene act on a dead body?"

That particular had haunted me in the hospital, too, and no TV show had given me a comfortable answer. "If somebody is desperate enough . . ."

"Let the dead be, Mr. Finley."

"Why, Governor? Because you don't want people talking about Tommy Reynolds anymore? Because there might be a messy trial involving people you know?"

"Wouldn't that be sufficient reason?"

"Hardly."

It was his idea of humor, and it passed as quickly as it had come. He decided it was time to pull out the speech. "From what I understand, you've looked into this matter a great deal. That's commendable for your line of work. But what you've probably also come across is one of the rare initiatives in this part of the country where people of substance have put their money where their consciences are. I'm not asking you to share their beliefs. I have grave reservations about their intent. But that's legitimate political difference, what makes the system work. More to the point is an active citizenry, a demonstration that the cynical Me-First years are behind us, that even the wealthiest of us realize he lives in a society filled with ferment and it isn't sufficient to with-draw to a mansion and watch one's money grow. There should be an active dialogue of opinions and interests. That's what this country is about. Otherwise, forget terrorist attacks. What we'll all be doomed to is what that poet said would be a whimper rather than a bang."

I tried to look impressed. But I wasn't and remembered I had an arm and a rib's worth more of an investment than he did.

"Yeah, but then that poet wrote a musical about singing cats, so he wasn't too worried about the whimper, either."

"That supposed to be funny?"

"No, it's supposed to be me pissed off. You want to pretend about something for my sake, that's one thing. But don't try to make me think you believe what you're saying. We're here to talk about covering the asses of your friends or acquaintances or whatever the hell they are to you, nothing else."

He thought it over. "There's that. But your speculation also happens to involve other innocent people. Excuse me."

I didn't know what was coming when he extricated his legs from the picnic bench and loped over to one of the doors, but I kicked myself for having ruled out too fast the possibility of some Rocco emerging from the room with a baseball bat. The kick turned out to be deserved, but for another reason: It was Mary Reynolds who walked out of the side room.

"Ms. Reynolds and I have had a long talk about this atrocious episode, Paul," he said, back to the grand manner. "It isn't much, but at least she's relieved you've helped bring her brother's killer to justice."

She was infuriating: She seemed to have an endless supply of pleated sun dresses, intimidated postures, and sad eyes. "We've got to talk, Mary. And not here."

She braced herself for her lines; unlike him, she seemed to believe in them. "Tommy was very young for his age, Mr. Finley," she said. "I think I told you that. Some people would like to believe the foulest things about him, but I know he was raped and murdered by that pervert. I just don't want to have to go on thinking about it every time I pick up a newspaper."

I told my arm to go to hell as I got up from the table. "Listen to me, Mary. They don't care about you. They don't care about Tommy. They want everything just to go away. They even want to keep Clary out there just in case they need him someday . . ."

Wrong button. "Richie was bad company for Tommy, Mr. Finley," she said firmly. "I don't care about him."

It was useless, and all three of us knew it. He suddenly felt relaxed enough to leave Mary standing by herself and to go back to the table to pour her a coffee. "Of course you realize there'll be changes at Gramercy," he said. "I believe the new claims man is named Kimberly. I've heard he admires your work a great deal. You're even together in one of these fantasy baseball league things, aren't you?"

I refused to take my eyes off her. If she wanted her only battlefield to be the private misgivings of her conscience, then I wanted her to know she had lost even there. She finally glanced out the window, and I had my miserable consolation prize.

"Mr. Stedina will drive you home," he announced.

"I'd prefer a cab."

"Well, we don't really want a cab coming here. Would you mind calling one for yourself at the harbor? It's only a few minutes' walk."

"My pleasure."

I got out without looking at either one of them again. Stedina was still behind the wheel and smoking. He said nothing as I trudged past him, and didn't know how lucky he was. If he had uttered a syllable, I would have told him how even the petty promises they had made to him about work weren't worth the air they had been written on.

At the harbor the gulls were still diving in the gray air. I did the convenient thing of cursing Mary Reynolds more than His Lordship, the Bakers, Chichester, Ellen Miles, or any of the other civic-minded citizens who were going to save the world from abortion clinics and then move on to whatever other cause their credit card souls told them was worth investing in. She was their rank and file, and she would lend herself to them even more mutely than someone like Walter Gregg ever had. At least Gregg hadn't thrown a brother into all the amnesia.

I had to wait 15 minutes at a hack stand for a cab. That gave me plenty of time to study the flotsam the gulls were so eager to pluck off the water.

CHAPTER 42

The first day, the Professor just heard me out about Richie Clary, throwing in periodic commercials that I was speculating. By the second day he had concluded that 48 hours out of the hospital without a hint of a new client was an omen for the rest of my life. He was so depressed by his conclusion that he brought along a book on the Weimar Republic to put between us on the supper table.

I left him to his Germans and tried concentrating on forking my cut up chicken with one hand. The fact of the matter was I did have to consider some practicalities. As long as I didn't call Kimberly—and I was sure they were all waiting for that move as a sign of my accepting the prevailing reality of things—I stood as much chance of attracting new clients as I did of renting a movie at the Star Video in the mall. That in turn made me think that maybe it was time to consider a more radical move, such as getting out of Garden City and moving to the city. How much longer was I going to share my cocoon with Joe Carroll, anyway? Was he even officially my father-in-law anymore?

As if he had read my thoughts, he peered up at me over the top of his book. "You should read more history," he said.

"So I won't be doomed to repeat it?"

"So you'll have something to do in your idle time."

"I'm thinking, Joe. I'm thinking."

"I know," he said, putting aside his book. "It's the decisions I'm worried about."

"I'm not close."

"But you're starting to measure the distance, right?"

"I'm a big boy. And you're a bigger one."

"And you're not ready yet, Paul. Impatience isn't wisdom, especially when you're broke."

Even my ferrets felt gnawed out; how long had he been waiting for me to get where I had arrived? "I was thinking of hitting you up for a few bucks," I said, actually thinking of it. "Just till I get settled."

"Always a possibility," he nodded. "But first things first. Your theory about how Tommy Reynolds died."

"What the hell's that got to do with this?"

"I think everybody should die once," he said sternly. "It's enough."

His explicit disapproval was harder to take than I had expected. "Think I don't know that? Who would I be doing it for even if I could prove it? His sister doesn't want to hear about it. Christ knows nobody else does."

"I wasn't just talking about Tommy Reynolds."

His stare waited me out until the penny dropped. He might as well have grabbed me by the neck and forced me to look away from Tommy Reynolds in the woods to Susan scrunched against the dashboard, the thinnest of hairs curved around to her mouth. "It has nothing to do with them, Joe."

"Good," he nodded. "I'm not saying that would've made your theory less plausible, but I don't need you going off the deep end here just for the sake of going off the deep end, either. Think about what you want to do. Contrary to popular myth, Rome *was* built in a day. But there was a lot of planning ahead of time."

For the rest of the evening we said nothing more about Tommy Reynolds or my larval plans for moving out. I was even enthusiastic about a ninth-inning rally that gave the Mets a win over the Giants. We toasted the victory with a beer, talked about the division flag on the horizon for Shea Stadium, then went to bed. I gave one final thought to the Eastern Division, went back to the image of Susan's broken neck in the front seat, and started sobbing. The tears came out of such remote places in my body that even my cranky ribs were surprised and couldn't stop them. My pillow said nothing when I informed it that my wife and daughter had been killed in a car crash.

CHAPTER 43

It was the Sunday _Times_ that made me notice something that hadn't penetrated before. The Long Island section carried a rehash of what it called DISQUIETING MURDERS IN NASSAU COUNTY. The text was the usual stuff about the latent stresses of ostensibly successful executives like Peter Piccolo and the violent acts that sometimes ensued. There wasn't an original word in the piece aside from the fact that Piccolo's father, the Bensonhurst baker, had been hospitalized with his own stress. What hit me as it hadn't before was the picture of Miles, Lancaster, and all the county officials at the press conference. WHERE THE HELL WAS HERB LEVINE?

I put the paper down for a second to go over all the obvious explanations. Levine had been on vacation that day. Levine had drawn an even hotter case. Levine hated press conferences. The answers, in order, were no way, there was none, and he _loved_ press conferences.

Al Chiozza's wife answered the phone with her usual tone of greeting her husband's juvenile playmate. The pandemonium in the background sounded like a late breakfast to which every branch of the family had been invited.

"Hey, Finley," Chiozza chirped. "I didn't know heroes were allowed to mix with the common people."

"I'm about to ruin your day, Al."

"No, you're not," he said, but more guardedly. "I just saw my nephew pour chocolate sauce on his cereal. _That_ ruined my day."

"True or false. Levine was taken off the Reynolds case."

There was nothing—just the sound of a father barking at some kid named Ralph for "not listening to your mother."

I decided that was a True.

"Okay. Second and last question. He wasn't taken off for being the asshole he usually is."

Only a second of silence this time. "Some cops are assholes and some assholes really like being cops. You want to trade me Martinez, give me a call. Otherwise, go in peace."

The click in my ear evaporated Ralph, Ralph's father, and the merry scene around the breakfast table. Two Trues.

And so?

I pulled out the phone directory without worrying about the so. Why bother doting on the fact that Herb Levine not only didn't owe me anything, but would never again be able to think of Howdy Doody without wanting to kill me? As ballplayers liked to say, that would have just been negative thinking.

I punched out his number and waited to have another receiver slammed down in my ear. Was somebody bugging my calls? It was too late to worry about that.

"Hello?"

"Herb? Paul Finley."

I let it settle for a second. When nothing happened, I figured I had nothing to lose by going for it right away. "I'm missing something, Herb. I think you can give it to me."

"That right?"

The thorny Levine was a familiar Levine. "Problem is, I don't know exactly what it is. But when I didn't see you at the press conference, I knew you had it."

"You got a lot of nerve, Finley."

I told myself not to make too much of a relatively reasonable tone. That might have gotten me into overly optimistic ideas about how, as much as he resented me, he resented Miles more for being his superior, for being a woman, or for not doing anything to keep him on the case. "I know that. And I'm not going to give you a lot of horseshit. All I'm asking is you point me in the right direction."

His breath went away from the receiver, and I cringed in anticipation of the bang. But there was no bang, only dead air and a distant voice from Portland or Seattle, then what sounded like an argument between clenched teeth much closer. I tried to remember what Levine's wife looked like, but couldn't come up with a face.

"Just for the hell of it? So you can feel better?"

The accusation came so abruptly I imagined for a second it was the Professor on the staircase. But it was Levine, sounding very much like his challenge was my last obstacle. "No," I said. "There's an old baker in Brooklyn who needs to know. Maybe even a couple of kids and an ex-wife. I think Chichester's enough for them to deal with for the rest of their lives."

Silence. And then more whispering. I didn't know which side I was supposed to be rooting for, so I didn't root for either, instead willing some of Jennifer's Zen blankness through the phone lines.

"There was no penetration," Levine said finally. "The kid wasn't raped. There was no evidence of anything but the crushed skull. Everything else was bullshit, and a pretty sloppy job. There's a report somewhere."

The click finally came. It didn't sound at all impolite.

CHAPTER 44

Nobody in federal prosecutor Dumbrille's office wanted to hear it, of course. Who knew how many of them also liked to play softball in Montauk? But sitting in Dumbrille's neat office, wondering whether he had an itch to salute every time he walked past one of the flags surrounding him, I knew he had little choice in the matter. He knew it, too, a couple of hours later when, following some strenuous phone calls, the authentic medical examiner's report on Tommy Reynolds was mysteriously messengered to his desk. The nice thing about a band of extortionists, high or low, is that at least one member always stashes the smoking gun somewhere for eventual self-defense. I didn't want to dwell on how Dumbrille seemed to know where to go for the stash.

I got permission to leave after he summoned two young agents and told them to be discreet about picking up Richie Clary and bringing him in for a few questions. I drove around for a while playing over the scene of the two Federales arriving at the Clary door, probably getting Richie's mother and hearing her ask what was wrong. Hadn't she and Richie and the rest of the family gone through enough over that horrible killing? No, one of the agents would have answered, thanks to the survival instincts of somebody in the medical examiner's office or more of that over-cleverness by somebody in the police department, DA's office, or Elks club, you haven't gone through anything yet. And all in the name of the murderer and arsonist Peter Piccolo—so that his father,

already dying anyway, and his ex-wife, already loathing him anyway, could feel a little better.

Driving didn't cover it. It was near eight o'clock when I parked
in front of the Dover and went inside. It seemed a natural choice:
It was within walking distance of home if I needed to walk and it
was where I had first listened to Piccolo's woes. The game was on
when I walked in, but it took only a couple of scotches to forget
about it. Somewhere around 10, the bartender came out with it
that he recognized me and asked if it was true that Piccolo had
once been a Dover regular. I told him I didn't have the slightest
idea and asked for another drink.

For the most part, I thought only about old movies. I made up
a game in which I wasn't allowed to sip my scotch unless I could
answer my own question. Name the gunmen in *The Magnificent
Seven*. Name four actors who had played Jesus Christ and four
who had played John the Baptist. Name five John Wayne movies
with Ben Johnson and Harry Carey, Jr. It wasn't that easy, and
there were stretches that I didn't sip anything for 15 minutes. I
could still take pride in my self-discipline.

Not that there weren't interruptions. The digital clock behind
the bar was a nagging reminder to imagine what phase of the
interrogation Clary had reached with Dumbrille. A recent divor-
cee with too much makeup named Anique told me her life story.
The bartender kept refilling the pretzel bowl as a warning that I
needed to eat something. But I managed to ignore the distractions well enough to figure out what Joanna, Tommy Reynolds,
Piccolo, and Richie Clary had in common. It went back to my
first conclusion about her that day at the pool: Joanna had been
waiting for something to happen to her. As had Reynolds by leaving his condoms and swizzle sticks where his sister would have
found them. As had Piccolo by setting his little fire and then
throwing me into the mix with that and Joanna. As had Clary
by probably confiding a little too much to those twins who had
accompanied him on his tour of the video stores and who would
almost certainly provide Dumbrille with an interesting tidbit or
two. The Bakers and Chichesters, on the other hand, didn't wait
for anything; they went out and did the scurvy happening first.

Was that what made them the special people the Governor felt obligated to intervene for? Was that what distinguished them from me, who also seemed to have been waiting forever for somebody to hand me a life?

It wasn't an uplifting thought, especially because, as Piccolo had said, they weren't special only because of their money. Because of their power, everything they did was special. Chichester had even called their groping of teenagers special features, and with a straight face.

Special features!!??

The digital clock said 11:15 when I said goodnight to Anique and to my drinking. I wouldn't have passed a police sobriety test, but I passed my own as I got into the car. Perched on my shoulder, the Professor said I was trying to close the circle altogether by getting into a collision. It wasn't the first time he was full of shit.

The nice thing about the grim street outside the Cameo was that few people dared to park on it., so I coasted into the space directly outside the theater. The marquee lights were already off, and the cashier was gone. A dim lobby light was reassuring: My good friend Boardman was touching up a poster. I hadn't come so far to be disappointed by the marquee, and I wasn't. The night's fare had been LOVE SLAVES, KATHY TAKES KANSAS, and, most important, SPECIAL FEATURES.

Boardman opened the glass door with a pained expression. "Don't tell me that broad's breaking balls again!"

I pushed past him with my good shoulder. Down to it, I didn't want to say anything that would make me look like a jackass in 30 seconds.

"Where you going?"

"Check out your special features, okay?"

"It's almost over! Come back tomorrow . . ."

I lost him in the first wave of strawberry deodorant and perspiration. It didn't matter. Upon the screen was what I had come to see. I should say on about half the screen. Even by amateur video standards, it looked like the work of somebody with a bad case of the DTs. The only thing clear through all the shaking was that the "actors" were still looking forward to the first time they would be eligible to vote. I had arrived too late to see if the clothes they had taken off were Bolero uniforms.

Boardman was back, and I didn't want him. "What the fuck's happening?" he demanded, so loudly I was sure he was trying to warn somebody.

There were the same seven or eight from my last visit, but this time without a giggling couple. I didn't dare hope to see a familiar face, but I hadn't come not to hope, either. I headed for the projection room, Boardman after me and looking over his shoulder to see if his warning had been heard. The projectionist, a pony-tailed dude more interested in his *Time* magazine than in our interruption, did nothing but move his feet out of the way. I knew nothing about projectors except that there must have been some button to turn them on and off. I found the right one just as the projectionist seemed to be having second thoughts about his indifference and Boardman was nearing hysteria.

"You can't do that . . .!"

"The house lights, where are they?"

Pony Tail looked at Boardman indecisively. He still didn't care about what was going on, but wasn't sure he should have displayed that in front of Boardman. Boardman helped both of us out by shifting over in front of a wall panel of switches. Luckily, he was a lover, not a fighter, so a single arm was enough to move him away and let me get at the switches. I kept flipping levers until every store in town must have been lighted.

There was grumbling from Boardman about calling the cops, but I was more interested in the grumbling coming up from the orchestra. On the other side of the spy window, the singles were staggering up from their seats like zombies brought back from the grave, doing their best to look animated when they zeroed in on the projection booth. One bald wrestler looked like he was going to complain to the chamber of commerce or tear down the booth piece by piece—whichever appealed to him more.

"You're fucking stoned, man! You better get the hell out of here while the getting's good!"

My last hope was the skinny guy sitting in the side aisle and apparently determined not to show his face. But I glimpsed enough of him to know he wasn't the Scarecrow or Willy Baker or Fred the publisher or anybody else I had seen in Montauk. For this mission, anyway, Piccolo had been right: I had gone out there on the wrong weekend.

"Finished now, man?"

I had caught myself hoping again: still a flagrant crime.

"You look a little over the top, man. Maybe you've been through a little too much lately. Know what I'm saying?"

He looked perfectly sincere. "What's your first name, Boardman?"

"Robert. Why?"

I thought of Chichester. "Like an old friend of mine."

"That's great, man." He was back to being insincere, thinking he was being subtle about nodding to the projectionist and flicking a couple of the switches back to their original position. "Makes it a smaller world, right?"

I had him squeezed up against the wall panel before I realized that was how I wanted him. Boardman, Robert did what Boardman, Robert should have done—sweat on his upper lip. "Why would they want to come here and see their home movies in this place?"

"Who? What the hell are you talking about?"

"Come on, Robert. The people who supply your special features. The ones who reduce your overhead, who have private reasons for keeping this place open. Why would they want to take their home videos here and see them in these sleazy surroundings instead of jerking off at home in their living room?"

Wisdom from the mouths of sleaze: I could feel it even before he told me. "It's bigger, man. Bigger everything. You can get really bored keeping it all private. We're talking about public people, right? That's what they're used to, what they expect. Why should I say no to a freebie from people like that?"

I was sorry the Professor wasn't there. He would have had to give an A to Robert Boardman.

CHAPTER 45

Thanks to Hanna, I knew the route from my car. In the moonlight, the pool looked clean and cold. I wanted it to be clean and cold. As I started throwing my clothes off, I could hear Richie Clary saying "please" to Dumbrille again and could hear Dumbrille clearing his throat to ask another lethal question. I could hear the word going out to the Governor, Miles and her husband, the Country Executive, and the Baker crowd about Dumbrille's arrogance in moving in on a county matter and what that might mean for them all.

Or maybe I was wrong, and Dumbrille was sitting in some back room with the Governor devising some new story to account for the panicky job Richie had done in trying to make Tommy Reynolds look like a rape victim.

The freezing water grabbed my balls and stomach. I tried not to yelp, then made just as much noise splashing in to get the impact over with. There was cold, there was ice, and then there was the pool water. It wasn't the water that had to do the accommodating, it was me.

A light came on in the bedroom above the patio. I didn't wait to see her looking out. I went down to the deep end, challenging it to feel like a deep end. It didn't: It felt like merely more artificial water under me.

She seemed to take forever to come downstairs and turn on the living room light. I saw her white terrycloth robe but didn't see her. I didn't have time for that.

I went down to the bottom where all pools look like pools and the mysteries of water buoyancy lose their mystery. The workmen I had seen that first day had done an impeccable job: The drains were spotless. Men had walked here before I had arrived, I reminded myself and had walked in work shoes.

I saw her shimmering next to the pool. She looked speculative. I wondered two things: how much my arm would hurt when I got out and which of us would admit first we weren't even sure we liked each other.

www.ingramcontent.com/pod-product-compliance
Lightning Source LLC
Chambersburg PA
CBHW030529020726
47494CB00004B/1273